LATENT CONTENT

RICK McGRATH

TERMINAL
PRESS

LATENT CONTENT

ISBN: 978-1-990682-19-3

First Edition
September, 2025

Published By
THE TERMINAL PRESS
Powell River, BC, Canada

Latent Content was first published in **Deep Ends** (The Terminal Press) 2022
White Out was first published in **Reports From The Deep End** (Titan Books) 2023
Spatial Psychology was first published in **Unauthorised Departures**
(The Terminal Press) 2024
The Icarus Incident was first published in **Unauthorised Departures**
(The Terminal Press) 2024

Front & Back Cover Art: Paul H. Williams

CONTENTS

LATENT CONTENT

Soon the final assault will begin. It's been just a few minutes since the bomb went off. After months of planning to finally have all the members of our video organization together for the first time I now realize it is only fitting the few of us remaining would record these precious moments for our millions of internet fans.

As I sit here — my left cheek burned with acid, my left arm broken by a monopod stick, and blood streaming into my mouth from a crushed nose — it occurs to me just how happy and proud we all are to stream this final episode of our undying respect for each other in such a dramatic, if expected scene of violence. I'm sure our many viewers will again bifurcate into camps of anger and joy across the globe.

I look at the cracked face of my cellphone. It now just fifteen minutes since 25 of my best employees — chosen from my video operations around the world — arrived here at this Spitalfields gallery to meet and greet each other after over five years of working together on the web. Disclaimer: when I say working together, I mean individually working for me.

The gallery in front of me is now silent after the bomb went off, save for the odd moan and shuffle of crawling bodies. My GoPro camera is still working, cleverly attached to the brim of my bowler hat, and I think the bodycam on my bulletproof vest is still operating.

Off to my left is the slightly twitching body of Prank Sinatra. He's on the floor about four staggers away, staring at me through blood-flooded eyes while he brandishes his camera and slowly inches towards me. The acid from his broken squirt gun has burned his right hand, which he holds up to his face like a cat licking a paw. A few feet away, lying on her back, her skimpy outfit slightly smouldering, SXT looks like she is trying to decide between passing out or reaching for a taser that lies just out of her reach. Her long legs are bruised, and I can see her rather remarkable breasts bear the imprints of many camera lenses.

Out cold along the wall beside me I spot FreeDom and Prince Abdullah Bey. FreeDom looks like he has taken some shrapnel, but I can see his chest still rising and falling, and he has a can of bear spray in his hand. The Prince is obviously struggling and has a bad cut across his throat.

Both lie in a mess of paper from Abdullah's ever-present file folder. Watching all from the hallway opposite is Paul, sitting safely with a laptop on his knees. The rest of the room is filled with overturned tables, splatters of food, broken bottles, smashed recording devices and the twisted bodies of my invitees, a brave, if unusual cadre of workers I will find difficult to replace, should I withstand the impending attacks of my patriotic lieutenants.

I now admit it was a risky decision to bring my executive staff and their minions together in person after years of digital interaction. But I felt the time was right for a final face-to-face. Over time our electronic relationships had evolved from strictly business to almost daily zoom calls of an increasingly personal nature — which finally led to what I thought were shallow, but mutually beneficial friendships. Well, as friendly as you can be with certified morons and narcissistic psychopaths. True, the business is mine, but when dealing with aggressive people with deeply stupid convictions, it's often best to show them some empathy — if it's useful. That's what I did and that's why I'm earning millions from my foray into the world of big streaming video channels — a fiscal fun ride that, as is often the case, started as a thing to do, an antidote to boredom. Think back. We all remember when smart TVs arrived years ago and the first thing everyone did was hunker down, drink more, and scan the internet. More correctly, do a full body dunk in the streaming video services that flowed like rivers in a rainforest and swept us all out to the Big See of companies like TikTok and YouTube.

YouTube was the most fascinating. What a business model: amateurs upload home movies and the company salts them with advertising, sharing a bit of the proceeds with the content providers. It didn't take long for a whole industry to emerge, with everyone from experts to rank amateurs setting up individual channels to flog, well, virtually anything you could imagine. As a retired code writer at a major software firm, it all looked quite simple — load up with a variety of cameras, microphones, and chose an appropriate shooting set, or work outdoors "on location." I chose to work indoors, and my initial plan was to talk about books from my extensive collection of 20th century science fiction.

My first video drew a crowd of zero viewers.

I had made some kind of technical error, it transpired, and my premiere podcast to the world played with no audio. I might have taken this embarrassment as perhaps a sign from the gods, or at least a wrist slap from Mister Think-About-It, but I had decided the world needed to see and hear from me about topics of questionable interest to all but the discriminating or esoteric viewer. That's what I told myself. In reality, I was running short of dosh and had heard ear-watering accounts of whiskey tasters, swimming pool enthusiasts, abandoned airport explorers, and an apparently endless stream of offbeat talking heads who were all making very good money, thank you, with proceeds from their clicks and views. Crafty YouTube, I thought, they've simply monetized home movies and tossed back what, a few pennies on each ad dollar earned? Well, I was ready for some of those pennies. But I needed clicks and views.

So, I kept at it. If at first, etc. I did a series of videos on my book collection. Yawn.

Then my favourite records. Better.

Then film noir movies. Yawn.

Then sporatic vids on anything I found interesting.

Yes, my viewership slowly grew, but plateaued out at around 500 subscribers and very few views. I was making pennies, all right, but barely enough to cover my eyes.

I needed a new approach. A little research revealed much. Generally speaking, YouTube videos offered information, persuasion, entertainment, and most of all, drama. Nearly all the popular content featured drama — usually revenge rants or compendiums of car crashes — and late one night as I watched a montage of angry people arguing with the staff at a big box store over shooting video of the interior, I decided to venture out with my spiffy new cellphone mounted on a selfie stick with a microphone attachment. It was easy: I dressed in black, wore a bowler, covered my face with oversized dark glasses, and walked around the streets recording everyone on the sidewalks until someone asked what I was doing. "Taking video," I would reply, pushing the camera up into their face. If challenged further I would announce, "There's no guarantee of privacy in public," and then hopefully get into an extended argument over citizen's rights with my hapless victim.

My viewing numbers grew. It was an adrenaline rush. I got a half decent payout.

Granted, most of the comments from my audience cheered on my increasingly aggravated harassments, but I also discovered a minority of viewers suggested I undertake even more psychopathic behaviour.

I decided to go out at night. I got lucky on my first midnight run in one of our more upscale neighbourhoods. I had been quietly wandering across lawns and shooting the interiors of homes that still had their lights on, my presence camouflaged in a black jogger's outfit and full balaclava. I had just come around a tall hedge when a group of teens appeared on the street. Reversing back into deep shadows I watched as they gathered around an expensive house and brazenly began to graffiti the doors of its two-car garage. It took but a moment to raise my camera and capture the meaningless desecration, and I had to stop myself from joining in on the fun.

I rushed home to post the video of this random act of vandalism and wasn't particularly surprised when my viewership virtually doubled as the event was picked up and shared across a variety of social media. I admit I was surprised when the police showed up a day later. Enthused as I was to post videos, I had neglected to fully read YouTube's rules and regulations about what could legally be shown. Criminal behaviour was banned, and the company was only too happy to answer questions from the authorities.

I fobbed off the cops with a story of how I thought my video would help bring the miscreants to justice, and that plus my standing as a solid citizen let me off with a warning. Not willing to risk jail time against my growing profits, I decided to go after YouTube on a technological level.

First off, I had to get around YouTube's algorithms for detecting inappropriate content. No more vandalism, swearing, nudity, or obviously illegal activities. The good stuff.

After a few days of study and numerous experiments I found I could set up an innocuous channel which would act as a feeder to direct my viewers to more exciting content, which, I hoped, would evade YouTube's never-sleeping bots. My approach was novel but simple: write a program that would disassociate the comments section from the actual video and then use that link to post my more exotic recordings ... hidden in plain sight.

My new channel was simplicity itself: I found and hired a single man who agreed to let me wire up most of his modest house with cameras. We left out the bed and bathrooms simply because I couldn't convince him it was all in the name of Art. He argued his name was Paul. He seemed to be at some medium level of autism spectrum disorder, which further suited my needs. I named the channel *Latent Content* and let it run continually for a month while I organized the money-making part of my plan.

As might be expected, my numbers dropped to almost nothing with *Latent Content*, and I'll be the first to happily admit watching Paul perform his daily rituals was about as interesting as staring at a cloudless sky. No matter, the stage was set and whatever happened next all future traffic would flow through this gatekeeper site. Yes, I was surprised to discover a few weeks later that Paul's timekeeper schedule in his modest home had attracted the interest of a few thousand boredom-enthused viewers.

My first hire was the wacky Prank Sinatra, a complete psychotic who terrorized the Manchester region. I offered him £2,000 a month to supply me with all his videos, which ran from minor pranks to more damaging stunts. His early recordings featured mostly puerile situations, such as leaning a barrel of wastewater up against a front door and ringing the bell. Or applying pepper spray to the doors of cars in a hospital parking lot. His shtick was to dress like the famous singer but use a metal kitchen whisk as a microphone. Who thinks of these things?

I carefully packaged up his work and simply added a link to it on *Latent Content*, utilizing my hide and seek software.

My final choice was a raunchy female who called herself SXT.

Within days Prank had generated a hundred thousand views, and possibly in response to the many comments for more he upped his game to include petty arson, obscene graffiti, and then a squirt gun full of either paint or bleach. It was brilliant stuff.

Prank was good, but my core group was rounded out in the good old US of Assholes, where I found a wide and often-confusing level of belligerence spread from coast to coast. After a week of judging over a hundred possible hires, I chose a so-called freedom of the press auditor in Alabama who called himself FreeDom, and a black sovereign citizen in Boston, who identified as a Moorish national, called Prince Abdullah Bey. My final choice was a raunchy female who called herself SXT, which she explained stood for Sex Times Technology.

She wandered around the western United States, concentrating on inflicting a wide and often-confusing level of annoyance from Seattle south to San Diego. A thirty-five-year-old from San Francisco, she had an obsession over the city's psychedelic past and had a drug-dealing hippie's deep aversion to anything authoritarian.

Her Grace Slick looks, tall, sexy body and throwback wardrobe — a loose tank top and red silk hot pants — generated a lot of male interest, but it was her insistence that she was a journalist, protected by the First Amendment, that made her famous as a must-watch video agitator. Well, that and her looks.

None expressed much interest in joining my growing company, but in true entrepreneurial style we worked out a program of base salary and bonuses for achieving certain viewership levels. I also agreed to cover any court costs.

The results were quite amazing, as they all picked up the pace of their operations and started sending me tapes on a daily basis. FreeDom was improbably popular. His usual routine was to enter a business with his camera running. He usually worked with another auditor who filmed the events from a distance, as the best vids offer multiple views. It was easy to get him kicked out of private property, so he moved on to quasi-public areas, like post offices, police stations, psychiatric hospitals, and animal shelters.

Here he harassed employees over his constitutional right to film as a journalist until he received trespass notices, and when the cops arrived he often resisted arrest. His female fans loved it. Called themselves DomBelles and had t-shirts printed up with his favourite sayings: "Call Your Supervisor" and "Am I Detained?"

I happily paid his legal fees, which never amounted to much as most civic prosecutors couldn't be bothered with paperwork-heavy simple misdemeanors when there were more tasty felonies about.

Prince Abdullah Bey was more expensive for me, but I still paid the court and vehicle towing costs associated with his claim he was a "sovereign citizen" and outside any federal or state laws. This, I thought, was pure cop-baffling genius. His videos were basically the same — he would be pulled over for either having no licence plate or a fake one — and then challenge the confused cop's jurisdiction, brandishing a briefcase of misinterpreted court decisions going back to a fictitious 1787 treaty between the United States and Morocco that grants Moors immunity from US law, and that he was The Prince of a legitimate country called Muur, and the USA was a ten-kilometer circle around Washington, DC. It was at this point the cops called for backup.

When asked for licence, registration and insurance Abdullah launched into his many-faceted yet specious arguments that proved he was not a "driver" but a "traveller" and therefore could freely go wherever. Because his "automobile" was simply private property and not used for commercial purposes he could not be subject to "contracts" between the state and an individual.

He claimed his Moorish passport — bought from the web — was all he needed to identify himself to the police.

He dressed somewhere between a circus clown and a Turkish prophet, from his red fez hat to flowing kaftan to leather Mughal shoes with long, curled tips. Depending on how busy the cops were, this argument could easily go on for a half hour or so before the frustrated officers broke his window, dragged him out, arrested him, and had his car towed. All gold.

SXT was equally prolific, harassing the public up and down the coast. Her routine was to patrol sidewalks, filming patrons at outdoor cafes, and obsessively haranguing any police that responded to calls of inappropriate behaviour. She also dabbled in the sovereign citizen shtick but had problems remembering the quasi-legal scripts that attempted to prove she didn't need a driver's license. The word salad rationale she spouted to the bemused police merely postponed her eventual arrest.

Her best idea was to set up our operations as a kind of pyramid scheme, with other auditors reporting to her and FreeDom, and then down an ever-expanding series of sub-lieutenants. Our operations expanded exponentially.

By this time my clicks and views were into six figures and my payout from YouTube was now quite substantial. Sounds good, but I had many expenses, in salaries, bonuses and legal fees. Then I had my best idea. Work the other side of the fence.

I had noticed for many months that while a certain number of viewers cheered my crew on to even more outrageous acts, there was a large audience that delighted in calling out the idiocy of these argumentative crazies. To cater to these malcontents, I set up another channel in which I replayed parts of my crew's videos and then mercilessly mocked them for their imaginative — if doomed — portrayals of these suburban dreams of violence.

I called this channel *The Frauditor*. Double your viewers, double the dough. I ran this enterprise separate from the now-bustling *Latent Content* channel, wisely deciding to not inform my workers of this new income stream and never showing my face onscreen. That may have been slightly paranoid on my part, as none of my contributors had ever seen a real photo of me — when pressed I used an old shot of a young, drunk, sneering Prince Andrew as my media avatar.

Over the next year my profits grew, and my prominent earners naturally became friendly with each other — passing on tips or provocative ideas — and SXT became quite convivial, suggesting I visit her in San Francisco and perhaps go out on a shoot with her as she increased her clickbait potential with bouts of public dope smoking around the Haight. It was tempting, but my success kept me busy at the home computer on Old Charleston Road.

That was to change.

I soon began to hear stories of unrest within the work force. Some of our less confident troops were complaining about being ridiculed by *The Frauditor* — I had shamed and humiliated many over their moronic actions and had ventured into making derogatory comments about their personal lives — and quite a few of our British crew had simply quit or gone back to their own money-losing, small time operations. I brushed aside all concerns, pointing out the increasing cash flow and never-ending stream of new belligerents to fill the gaps. Plus, I reminded them, *The Frauditor* channel was also promoting our content, if in a backhanded way.

FreeDom was not convinced. SXT was suspicious. Prank Sinatra threatened to leave. The Prince decreed an investigation. Sensing there was more than potential trouble brewing, I agreed to meet with them. Personally. In order to grasp this toad by the horns I suggested we do a quick poll of the top producers and see if any future date would be amenable to us all. Was I surprised when it became apparent any date is good when you're basically self-employed? No. We settled on a date two weeks hence, which I changed to a month when I saw the cost difference in first class British Airways seats. All agreed.

The general plan was simple. I had placed my 25-odd guests in various hotels around east London, and at noon the next day my hopefully jet-lagged digital friends would all meet at my rented warehouse. The morning of the grand event I arrived early to set up some decorations, including festive banners celebrating the boredom of *Latent Content* and the triumph of our circumventing YouTube's rules of publishing anti-social content. Tables were set out with examples of fine Sussex wines, Cheddar Gorge cheeses, and of course, traditional English fish and chips. I also attended to some special preparations in case my attendees reverted to form.

The group had taken their time arriving at the building, as the auditors filmed all the pedestrians and police they met along the way; SXT scandalized a group of Japanese tourists, all of whom took photos of her; Prank sprayed fluorescent paint on the backs of unknowing executives on their way to work, and the rest caused general mayhem with cabbies, bus drivers, and car rental clerks. They were all substantially wound up by the time they made it to the gallery.

The agenda for our first meet-up was simple and straightforward. The troops would assemble at a respectful distance, and I would go through the general business of a convention. Welcome all, recognition of outstanding efforts — highest profit, most bonuses — an overview of clicks and views, and finally plans to infiltrate the more difficult markets of India and Asia. A quick Q&A and then into the food and drink. I even had a heavy metal rock band organized and some actors dressed as cops to antagonize the American contingent.

Everyone arrived at almost the same time, and each group brazenly entered the room, dressed in their video personas, carrying a variety of cameras, microphones, selfie sticks, and pepper spray. A beautiful sight. We all happily filmed each other as a sign of mutual respect. The event was being streamed live for our legions of viewers.

I began as planned, and had gotten well into the recognition phase when I became aware of a commotion at the back of the crowd. One of my auditors — from Miami, I think — was claiming I was, in fact, their greatest enemy, the person behind *The Frauditor*.

"Hold on," I called out. "Calm down. That's crazy." This wasn't going to plan.

A tall black kid held up his cellphone. "This hacker pal of mine says *Latent Content* and *The Frauditor* use the same IP address. Both are yours!"

I could sense unrest rippling through my audience.

"Don't be a dimwit halfwit nitwit," I yelled back. Big mistake. I had blurted out one of my favourite *Frauditor* putdowns.

There was a gasp from the group.

"You called me a fucking stupid ignorant whore that got ripped off because tits aren't brains!" SXT pointed her red iPhone at me. She extended the handle of her metal selfie stick.

The crowd started making grumbling noises.

Prank shifted to my left and moved towards me along a buffet table. I noticed his hand grabbed an implement.

"How much are you making off *Frauditor*? Call us names and pocket the ka-ching, right?" Prince Abdullah took off his fez and pulled a small canister of pepper spray from the inside.

The jig appeared to be up. I backed off a few steps, and the mutineers advanced upon me, cameras bobbing with their steps. Prank got close enough to stab my left side with a cheese knife as I pepper sprayed his eyes and pushed him back, and SXT managed to whack me heavily on the arm with her selfie stick before I kicked her back onto the floor. She fell heavily.

A full-frontal attack by all was averted when some of the crowd started fighting among themselves. Two brave, if misguided defenders of my innocence began circling my accusers, screaming out "don't touch me" and fumbling for their personal weaponry.

Attention was diverted. This was my chance. Time for Plan B. When the crowd started to separate into warring camps, I gave a yell, pointed over their heads, and pushed a button on my cellphone. There was a loud bang and a panel in the ceiling opened, sending a shower of crisp £50 notes to the floor. Those closest to the ensuing snowfall of cash bent over and tried to grab the money one-handed while working to keep their cameras pointed at me, and soon most of my junior executives were scrabbling around on their haunches, fumbling for bills while attempting to film the frenzied scene.

During the melee I curled into my balloon chair — the actual white chair used by No.2 in The Prisoner TV series, which I had planned to give away as a door prize — turned it away from the crowd and hit a second button.

Small but potent charges of plastic explosives detonated under various strategic parts of the floor. Bits of oak planking cut through the confined space like shrapnel. Everyone within a few yards of each blast was instantly killed, and the shock waves blew everyone else to the walls of the room. Many died when their cameras, always at eye level, penetrated their skulls. My four closest associates — already rich and more interested in attacking me than chasing notes — were furthest from the blast and thankfully survived. Pleased to have been cleansed by Prank's acid and SXT's now-broken monopod, I had been further blessed by a bit of glass from a blown-up camera that had bounced off the wall and caught my nose, but otherwise I was still capable of a good fight.

As the smoke cleared, I see Prank and SXT shooting their final videos for posterity. Prank is trying to blindly crawl towards me on his elbows and knees. His right hand is burned and bloody, in the other his cellphone is weaving about like he's a blind man performing sign language for the dead. SXT, despite her burns and injuries, has overtaken Prank and has her mangled monopod poised above his head for a final strike. She is already thinking ahead for the best way to overcome my defensive position. I haven't shown her my taser. Yet.

Off to my right I see Prince Abdullah Bey and FreeDom seem to have died in a mutual embrace of First Amendment mania. Both had stuffed pages of irrelevant Supreme Court cases down each other's throat.

I look over the mayhem of broken furniture and scattered bodies to the hall and see Paul in his chair, sitting quietly with my laptop on his knees, tuned into both *Latent Content* and *The Frauditor* channels. I give him a hand wave and he flashes back a double thumbs up... confirmation this live broadcast is being watched by the most viewers we've ever attracted.

As I survey the carnage and film the last moments of my mutinous colleagues, I once again thank them for their support of my video channel, and silently praise their alternate worlds and the powerful imaginations that built them.

ADMAN

My name is Pete Russell, and I'm a copywriter. You know, one of those guys who writes those ads you love to hate. That's OK by me, because you have to remember 'em to hate 'em. That's what I get paid to do. Just sit around and daydream, usually with my partner, Stu Davey, the art guy. I think up the concepts and he does the visuals. That's the way it's supposed to work. Division of labour crap.

Actually, we both do everything at the beginning. It's sorta cool. Here's how it goes. We meet with the agency's creative director, and the account guy who's assigned to suck up to the client, and maybe somebody from the media department.

The account guy — we call him a Suit cause he has to wear one to look like he means business with his clients — the suit gives us the briefing. Yeah, Suit sounds derogatory, but we all have our little nicknames. Artists are known as Wrists, and writers are called Typists. Fun business.

Suits are always fascinated with a load of info about the product we gotta sell, what's so great about it, who's most likely to buy it, how much dough we can spend producing our ideas, and, most importantly for Stu and me, how long we've got until he tries to sell our concepts to the client.

It's all MBA marketing crap and we just sit there and take it all in, like we're enjoying his rap and we believe all his numbers and psychographics and studies will make a difference. Yeah, it's probably important, but only for oddball target groups. We're the good humour men.

I work on three accounts, so I've got three suits to deal with, and Fred Johnson's the best for playing this game. He doesn't like the creative guys, can't figure out why we tick, and he likes to write out all the marketing shit on a whiteboard in different colours as he talks out his fantasies of perfect results.

Then we hear a little lecture — or is it a sermon — from Robert R. (Bobby) Hunter, the agency's creative director. Some vague ideas about "brand personality" and what he calls the "integrity of creative," whatever that means. He's a stuffy Brit from the Saatchi office in London — that's bigtime here in Toronto — and the story of why he's here and not there might be interesting, if you cared.

Stu and I figure he's still uncomfortable with adjusting to creativity in the colonies. And Canadian accents don't tell snooty Englishmen much about our backgrounds. Still, he's a bigtime guy in the biz, CD of one of Canada's most profitable agencies, and he's gotta justify the big bucks he pulls down every year for telling us what ideas he likes. And doesn't.

My partner Stu's a funky guy, a wacky art director with his cowboy boots and flamboyant western shirts, and like most of his ilk, is a regular fanatic about The Look. Well, it matters. He's a print specialist. The cowboy touch is a bit corny for 1985, but he pays it off with a totally western motif office, with posters of oldtime movie cowboy stars and Roy Rogers lunchboxes and an Apache rug on one wall.

He first went western in Vancouver, working for some local agency, and they started calling him Tex, a name only a few of us use these days, usually when we're drunk.

So, we do the briefing and then Stu and I usually split to a quiet bar, like the *Scotland Yard* down on Front Street, drink some beer, watch the unemployed play some darts, and bullshit about solutions to our little problem.

A lot of people think we get our ideas in a sort of "aha" instant insight. That's Hollywood. Oh yeah, sometimes you get a great idea right outta the blue, but mostly it's just the opposite. Mostly it's fuckin hard work with a brutal deadline and a lot of unimaginative suits breathing down your neck for something, anything, they can flog to the guys who pay the bills.

But Stu and I have our standards. True, we're often obnoxious at the briefing, but that's usually just to tick off the account boys. You wanna know the usual technique? I'll tell you. It's called thinking up every goddam idea you can, deciding it doesn't work and throwing it away.

By a process of elimination you end up with something that works. Pure reductive thinking. Which is probably why we like the *Scotland Yard* as a pub. Reminds us of Sherlock, who would have made one bitchin adman. Maybe.

You get into a time-free zone. The agency is busy, as usual, but it's white noise to me. I'm on a roll, like I usually am in the morning. It's one of the times I focus best during the day. Night is different. And a lot of my work doesn't involve Stu.

My IBM Selectric is just humming as I pound through a series of 30 second radio spots for a big bedroom furniture retailer. Surprised? Don't be. Most of the stuff we do is the non-glam shit that simply moves product. Gets the asses in the store.

I had my fun with this account last fall when we picked up the business and I blew them away with my "Great in Beds" campaign for their line of various waterbeds. The sales staff all sported "I'm Great In Beds" tee shirts and we paid it off with radio and print. Yes, the billboards of a buxom girl on a waterbed did push good taste a tad. Hey, it's waterbeds. Push once, rest two.

Now it's spring break sale time, and my theme is "Sofa, So Good" with increasing price breaks every day of the week. Dutch auction goes retail. Around 11:30 my phone's intercom beeps and Stu's sotto voice creeps into my office.

"Boom-boom, Boom-boom," he drones, doing the opening notes to *Alzo Sprach Zarathustra*. "You called?"

"Bring the RBC/Oulter boards, Stu, Booby's waiting."

"Be right over."

Booby's the career-terminating nickname Stu and I coined for Bobby, the agency's creative director. We gave him his rather unflattering sobriquet after noticing his strange nervous tick of scratching his right nipple between the thumb and index finger of his left hand.

At first I thought he was oddly itchy, but it's just his way of dealing with the kind of stress you experience when

you're in unfamiliar territory. He was also somewhat overly attentive to any big boobed employee, and we also liked the way it fit into his last name: Booby Hunter.

He's an older sonofabitch, which can be a problem in this youngster's biz, but he was hot in his day, hot when everything was great during the creative breakthrough of the late 1960s, when the idea was king and great ideas could sell little shitboxes like Volkswagons and big shitheads like Nixon, but he went dry... like we all will. You just lose contact with the present. Not great when you need to make metaphors of the near future. His main concerns are business contacts, client lunches, and expense accounts. And he also decides if your ideas are any good.

Today he wants to see some roughed up TV storyboards for next September's RBC/Oulter Investments campaign. We're ready to rock.

Stu and I head to the meeting room. It's empty. Stu arranges the boards on the easel, and I adjust the overhead lights. This is the part where we sell ourselves. Booby arrives with Johnson the Suit and a secretary.

Booby's dressed in his usual: expensive blue sports jacket, Hathaway shirt, light sweater, gray slacks, Guccis, and patterned socks. He pulls back a chair and sits at the head of the table. His secretary hovers nearby.

"Greetings, Peter. Stu. Do you wish any coffee?"

"Sure, thanks." I look at Stu and he nods affirmative.

"Frederick?"

"No thanks, Bob, I've got a lunch at one. Don't want to kill my appetite."

"Be a sweetheart, please, Betsy. Three coffees. Thanks."

Johnson finds a chair and opens his file folder. Booby's already fiddling with his tit.

"All right now, gentlemen, let's begin. Frederick, perhaps we should begin with your review."

"Thanks, Bob. Now, as you know, this is our first major

campaign for RBC/Oulter." He gave me a this-is-important look.

"Strategically, RBC/Oulter is fairly well-placed among the country's top five investment banks, but their retail division has been taking a beating lately, especially from Reilly Securities and Leiningen/Wright Investments. Our research head, Greg Riley, predicts many of these firms will be swallowed up by major banks over the next ten years, and the brass at RBC/Oulter wants to be well positioned to cash out when that day arrives. The firm is a trusted name, with a good reputation, but their market share is stagnant and their recall numbers outside of large centres is very poor.

As you know, growth in the securities business is essentially based on reputation and brand name identification, but our biggest problem with RBC/Oulter's ideal primary target group is that they're composed of what I like to call the Lost Generation..."

Booby put up his hand to stop him as Betsy brought back the coffees on a tray. "Cream and sugar? Help yourself." Stu and I grabbed a cup each and leaned back as Johnson resumed his droning rap.

"Yes, the Lost Generation. Those people who should have been born between 1930 and 1945 but were denied their existence by the fact very few North Americans married during the great depression and the war."

"Guess that sort of makes it the great digression, eh?" I said. Stu giggled.

Booby gave me a squinty-eyed look.

"Don't give me your depressing humour, please, Peter. We're not here to waste valuable time. This is a short meeting. Frederick, ignore that remark, please. The floor is still yours."

The suit rifled through his notes.

"OK, what we want to present to the client is a double-edged sword. One that will cut to the quick in a hard-working campaign that delivers not only the 55- to 74-year-old males, but impacts favourably on the secondary group, the leading edge of that delicious lump of soon-to-inherit Baby Boomers.

"Media wants TV and outdoor, TV for the strong intrusive message, outdoor for the frequency factor. It's got to hit hard, and measure strongly for us to get them to approve phase two of the media buy. That's about it." He put his notes back in his file folder.

Booby slurped his coffee.

"Thank you, Frederick. Succinctly put, as per usual." He turned to Stu and me.

"So, chaps, what award-winning ideas do you have to make Frederick happy and still solve all our client's business problems?" Booby leaned back in his chair and pulled out his limited edition Montblanc pen, another of his affectations. It was filled with green ink.

Stu positioned himself by the easel while I walked around the table. I like to move while I talk. Booby and The Suit stared at the easel and the covered artboards. Nothing like a little suspense.

"Freddy is right," I began. "This campaign has proven to be a difficult problem. A very difficult problem." I saw Stu smiling out the window. We solved this one after just one joint and three beers.

"Not only have we been asked to deliver our message to people who, in fact, were never born, but we must expect these unborn souls to invest their unlife savings."

The suit was starting to turn the colour of Booby's ink. The Great Man was smiling, but just.

"Yes, Peter, yes, certainly a challenge of historical significance. But how do you propose to overcome this ethereal resistance?"

It was the perfect setup, and I silently thanked the Boober for his timing. I turned and looked the suit right in the eye.

"How do we create the perfect Excalibur, Freddy?

With mythological significance, of course! Selling advice is tricky, but we do have one huge advantage — the one great emotional button shared by all our target groups — their neurotic associations with money. Emotions, baby.

"Essentially, it boils down to two sides of the same ethereal coin: fear and greed. The fear of losing what you have when the markets tank, and the greed that envelopes you when markets skyrocket. The trick is to flog fear of losing to the older guys, who are already cramming for their finals and can't afford to speculate, and flog greed to the under 50s, who want lots of dough to set up whatever retirement fantasy we can sell them before it's too late. But we have to maintain our *integrity of creative* so we still project safety while promising intelligent returns."

Booby smiled. Stu coughed.

"Stu and I propose we do this with an historical theme, by comparing the financial genius of RBC/Oulter Investments to great moments of genius throughout western civilization. Stu?"

Stu flipped up the covering sheet on the first board and turned it towards Booby and The Suit.

"This first spot is called 'Eureka,' and it's based on Archimedes' famous discovery of the water displacement principle. We open with a long shot of Archie in his bedroom, wrapped in a towel. The voice over sets up the premise that all throughout time, certain genius types made important discoveries by having a special kind of superior awareness."

Stu started flipping his cards.

"After a series of cuts of toy boats floating, Archie entering the water, and the corresponding rise of the tub water, we hear 'Eureka' and Archie, wrapped now in a housecoat, runs down the hall holding a wooden boat. We end with a retired couple lounging in their swimming pool. A wooden toy boat bobs between them.

"A wise-sounding narrator reminds us that RBC/Oulter

sees significance in situations others take for granted, and you can profit from that kind of insight. We've done the same script for Galileo, Newton and Einstein. Each with a different target group ending. Stu is working on those cards. Well, whaddya think?"

Booby looked at Johnson. The little Suit was obviously pleased.

"Very good, boys, very good. I like it. Better still, I think the client will like it. Do you have it for billboards, too?"

Stu revealed another artboard. It showed a young Newton, lounging under a tree, smiling at a golden apple. The headline read: *The Ability to Catch What Others Miss.*

"Yes, good. Not too specific, not too obscure." Fred was smiling. "Bob, you approve?"

Booby nodded with enthusiasm.

"Certainly, Frederick, the boys have worked up a real winner here. Next we'll get production do a detailed costing, but I'll wager we can bring the TV spots in, with good talent, for about fifty thousand each. Well within budget. When do you want to present?"

"Sooner is always better. When Stu is done I can get research to pretest them in a focus group, then we'll tidy them up and make the pitch. Just one problem, though."

"Oh? What's that?" Booby's hand started creeping up to his chest again.

"The Einstein spot. Could have problems with that. Who really knows what he was talking about, and, well, ah .... there's that atomic bomb stuff."

"Bull" I said. "We've got a whole riff on relativity ... part of the pitch on Boomer wealth transfer."

Booby got out his green pen. "Frederick is right. A tad too esoteric and obscure. Rethink it. There's lots of other big name genius types out there. Maybe somebody Canadian."

"Good idea," Freddy added.

"Simon Fraser," Stu suggested.

"Norman Bethune," I said.

Booby was not impressed. "Not Scots explorers, Stuart, think Canadian."

Fred looked at me and rolled his eyes. "We'll leave the commie doc alone, too." He looked at his watch. "OK, twelve fifteen, gotta run. Work on it. Maybe one of those guys who cured diabetes." He flapped his folder under his arm and disappeared into the hallway.

Booby stood and adjusted his jacket. He put the pen away. "Nice idea, crummy presentation. Why do you chaps persist in mocking Frederick so? He's not a bad suit, really. Gets along very well with the clients. Could be a man to watch."

Stu and I both made like we were studying our watches.

"Enough, enough. You heard the man. Late next week for pre-testing. Stuart, dress the boards up a bit and we'll give them to Frederick Wednesday afternoon. Cheers, lads, have a good weekend."

Stu looked at me like he wishes he was the writer, and I smile back with the grin of someone who doesn't have to do any more work that day.

"Not that this will interfere with my usual weekend activities," Stu smiled. "I have it all set up with that new bimbo in trafficking. Told her I would do her portrait. In the nude. She said OK. Yowsers."

I give him my best look of disbelief. "Good for you. I'm beating the traffic outta here. Heading north to a very cozy cottage for a very quiet weekend of solid, solitary R&R. I'm gonna do some writing, catch up on some reading."

He gave me his best look of disbelief.

"So… lunch… shall we chow down?"

I laughed and grabbed my coat.

SPATIAL PSYCHOLOGY

Later, as he sat on the balcony poking the dying embers in the rough fire pit, Dr Robert Maitland reflected on the unusual events that must have taken place within this huge apartment block over the past year. Impressed by the building's size, with its forty floors and thousand flats, swimming pools and supermarkets — all now but abandoned to the sky — he was also surprised of not being aware of its existence until two days ago.

Formerly a young, brash experimental architect in a London design group — before he was injured in a serious car crash — Maitland used his lengthy time in recuperation to study Spatial Psychology, quickly earning his PhD by age 30 and making his name three years later with a seminal study of urban unrest in London's Chelsea district, where residents suddenly transformed their upscale neighbourhood into a scene of group self-mutilation, disguised as uncaring dereliction. The media was fascinated. Once a Chelsea resident himself, Maitland famously described the situation in his breakthrough *Guardian* series as an "event in Localized Spontaneous Decharacterization" — LSD. Basically, it was a violent, yet innately positive reaction to high levels of cultural homogenization within a confined geographic area.

Maitland followed this success with a regular output of well-publicized popular essays on the psychology of architecture, an ignored book on shopping mall parking lots, and an acclaimed study of internment camps in China.

Back in the UK after a year travelling, he had just completed his research on a bizarre group hallucination in a small town south of Heathrow. Now relaxing in a London bar, he was comfortably chatting with his old friend Richard Pearson, once an advertising executive his firm had hired to promote a new kind of small city car, and now the London sales manager for a major pharmaceutical company.

"No, no, no, Richard, really, for no apparent reason. That's the interesting part — well, the part I have to figure out." Maitland wove his wine glass in a small figure eight in front of him. "I was there for months. The population thought they were living in a tropical paradise, some thought they could fly, and a few found it impossible to leave. I walked around, interviewed the residents, and they all reported basically the same series of events. Damn puzzling."

Richard laughed in disbelief. "They thought Shepperton was transformed? Into a jungle? Brilliant! Christ, I could have used that idea at the Metro-Centre. Are there bears in the jungle? But Shepperton. I've been there, Robby — movie studios are big clients for our products. Sure, some places are crazy. That big loop in the river — betcha that's it. Perfect subject for a whatever-it-is spacey shrink like you."

Maitland smiled.

"Spatial, Richard, spatial psychologist. Maybe an architecturologist. Ever wonder why open plan offices are managed by psychopaths?"

"You're making that up. I run an open off — ahh, you bastard."

Maitland smiled again.

"Still, Richard, Shepperton doesn't fit the model evident in Chelsea or those nasty Japanese camps. Too much diversity. This could be a whole new area of interest for me. I'm hopeful. Unfortunately, the initial mania has slowly subsided and now no one seems to remember anything, save some crazy pilot they fished out of the river. And now he's disappeared. I don't know, sadly. Seems like they all had the same dream. Again, impossible."

It was Pearson's turn to smile.

"A washout, you say? Enthusiasm dampened? River of regret? Never mind, you'll think of something. In the meantime, I've got a little research tip for you, Roberto. This is right down your street. Or maybe hallway. What would you think about a large group of well-off people living in a self-wrecked building? Living there and liking it? This monster high-rise I know went from new and sold out to broken and abandoned in just over a year. Nobody bitched. Money just blown. Sorta creepy and cool in that psycho way you like."

Maitland was indeed interested. A vertical Chelsea? "Where?"

"Eastside, down by the river. Where it makes that big jog before London airport."

"And people still live there?"

"Apparently. Dunno. Maybe. There are stories. I don't cover that area anymore. Thankfully. Hey, you like a coincidence. Here's one. Didn't you write a paper a few years ago on that arsehole architect, Anthony Royal?"

Maitland rolled his eyes. Yes, he had. *Royal Revealed: King of Koncrete.* The brutalists had hated it.

"Well, get this. Anthony Royal designed and lived in that high-rise."

Maitland's eyes flicked sharply under his dark brows, Patrick McGoohan-style. "You know Anthony Royal?"

"Yeah, I know him. Don't look so amazed, Robert. We played at the same tennis club before Tony hit the ..." Richard lowered his voice, "... ahh, terminal beach. But that's not the story."

"Royal is dead?"

"Where ya been, Robby? His obit ran months ago. Oh,

yes. Obsessed in Shepperton. No London papers? All right, there's more." Richard looked around as if people might be eavesdropping. "It was just over a year ago I bought an flat in this new high-rise — on Tony's advice — as an investment, mind you — and I rented it to some TV producer and his family. He was a big, boisterous bastard but his wife seemed competent. Children. No matter. His rent cheque cashed the first month, but not the next. Or the next."

Richard took a slow drink to emphasize the gravity of this omission.

"I phone. No answer. Leave messages. No answer. So, Christ, I drive over to see what's the problem and am stunned by the condition of the building. Hell, it's only been open a few months and it's already breaking down. Lifts out. Dead animal in the swimming pool. Drunks fighting. My tenant is nowhere to be found. I'm pissed off. So are most of the people yammering at the superintendent.

"The fast lifts are still working so I head up to Tony's penthouse to confront the great man. We're in his glass studio. I'm ranting. He's looking ragged — there's all these white birds screaming overhead — and he appears to have no answers for what's happening on the floors below him. I finally mention my lawyer, and — hard to believe — right away he goes over to his desk and writes me a cheque for more than what I paid. Take it, he says, this place is a zoo. I look at his big, white Alsatian.

"Being a practical man, I took the money, signed some papers, and got the hell out. I wanted a long-term investment. Fast payoff! This was a year ago — looks deserted now — no doubt any inhabitants are squatters."

"Fascinating. But I don't believe in coincidences." Maitland finished his wine, caught the barman's eye. Maitland knew Pearson, like all salesmen, tended to exaggerate. "Are you sure the whole place reacted? The lower floors usually instigate the brunt of change first. I'm not interested in slums."

"How about this, then?" Richard adopted his face of adman sincerity. "When I was repping the new medical facility near the complex I dealt with one of the doctors who lived in the high-rise. Neurologist, if I remember. Maybe not. What was his name? Langley? No. Laing — that was it. He taught and ran the dispensary. Ordered all the drugs. Got to know him a bit — lived around the middle of the high-rise — floor 24 or 25. He was a tad odd."

"Odd?"

"Let's say unusual — hah ... why would you become a doctor to teach? But I started to wonder after dealing with him — they used a helluva lot of drugs. Heavy stuff. Morphine, mostly. Hey, maybe they had a cancer clinic out back. And when I called for an appointment he was rarely there — when we did meet he looked increasingly shabby, distracted, and, somewhat sadly, a tad ripe. I had to wonder."

"Did he complain?"

Richard snorted in his martini. "Just the opposite. He looked like hell — beardy and thin — but seemed quite content. That sorta dreamy thing, the long stare. His personality changed, too — from a sort of mousey voyeur type to something more self-confident — like a lonely adult becoming a popular teen. Again, I wondered."

"Did he talk about the building?"

"Rarely. He once called his home 'the cave on the cliff,' but he basically talked business and seemed quite anxious to return to the high-rise after our meetings."

The following afternoon Maitland drove down to the Thames and made his way east through an interzone of abandoned warehouses, communication towers, and auto wrecking yards.

He drove carefully and soon approached a gigantic high-rise, rising above a sea of rusting, smashed cars and a shoreline of indeterminate garbage, a dune of forgotten yesterdays in sun-faded plastic bags.

Off to the right another completed building was dark but not apparently deserted, and seemed to be covered in camouflage, until it became clear the discoloured streaks were the result of smoke from a series of balcony fires. Some clothing fluttered in open windows. Between these two were three half-completed towers, forming a rough semi-circle. He turned back to the primary target.

The entrance to the high-rise consisted of a path through a maze of wrecked furniture, faded and warped in the sun and rain. The big front doors were chained at the handles, but an adjacent window had been smashed and Maitland stepped into what appeared to be the main hall of an atrocity exhibition.

There's war in hell, Maitland thought as he carefully picked a route through the flotsam that almost completely covered the floor. He surveyed the carnage. The lifts were defaced with graffiti, bones littered the floor, and blood flecked in arcs over walls already defaced with crudely painted instructions and unintelligible threats.

Moving towards the emergency stairs, Maitland checked the lifts — none of the doors would open and a vaguely sweet putrid smell increased with proximity. Sludge was seeping under the deeply scratched and dented stainless steel doors. He tested the fire escape doors — they opened, and he made it up one floor before being stopped by a massive structure of intertwined furniture, smashed TVs, twisted bathroom fixtures and what looked like a car's rear bumper. He tried a few pulls and was about to try and dismantle the beaver-like dam when he heard what might have been a low growl from above. He retreated to the lobby.

What to do next, he wondered. The blocked stairwell. The distinct possibility of wildlife. The obvious signs of violence. *This was better than he expected*. Figuring this could be more complicated than simply exploring another abandoned building, Maitland decided to return home to his

Spitalsfield flat and prepare for a proper exploration of the high-rise the next day.

As he pulled away from the building his eye caught a sudden motion in the rearview mirror. Something on a balcony around the 10th floor. A figure in blue, wrapped in a red blanket?

Back on the road, Maitland drove north and was soon back in familiar territory. An idea occurred. He knew the manager of the local HM Land Registry and decided to stop in for a quick meeting. Once home he cleared a table, opened the just-obtained tube of blueprints, and began to study Anthony Royal's original plans for the high-rise project. He had analyzed Royal's other buildings in the past and — if the architect was true to form — somewhere in the overall design there would be an unidentified passageway Royal could use for covert access and egress. Tony liked his privacy. And there it was. A small area in the angle between two walls of the public and service lift shafts. He smiled. Happy ending.

When Maitland arrived on site early the next morning the warm June sun was butter yellow above the horizon and the three unfinished high-rises were backlit like the black stumps of a dog's broken teeth.

This time he was prepared — along with ample food and water he packed a heavy torch, wire cutters, narcotic-laced dog biscuits, some rope, and his favourite toy, a set of lock picks. Again, he carefully made his way through the lobby debris and then stopped short. Today a strange apparition dressed in a black cassock sat slouched in a broken chair in front of the fire stairs. A resident? When he got closer Maitland realized a dog's head had been crudely attached to a mannequin's shoulders. So, Anubis guards the stairs — fine. Not going in that direction, anyway. He turned left and made his way through the administrator's office to the back of the lift shafts.

...a smallish man dressed in a torn and stained Superman costume, with the furry remains of an Alsatian's head for a hat...

He explored a conundrum of service corridors and empty storage areas before he found a battered steel door, inset in the concrete behind a stack of smashed TVs. He knew the lock, and the door was soon opened to reveal a narrow set of circular steps twisting skyward beside a small, two-person lift. He looked up. There was a hint of light at the top of the shaft. He gingerly stepped inside the lift and was somewhat shocked to note the floor indicator light was illuminating "G." Was the power still on after all this time? He tentatively pressed 10 and was rewarded when the door closed and the lift slid quietly upwards. He felt a twinge of youthful excitement.

At the 10th floor Maitland exited the lift, carefully opened the service door and stepped into one of the high-rise's machine rooms, now a kind of psychedelic pasta palace, with various pipes bent in great arcs and others ripped from walls and ceiling, some of them decorated with lengths of different coloured electrical cord. A dentist's chair sat in one corner. This room led to more hallways and then into the Concourse area, spread out end to end in the high-rise like shops on a High Street.

After a brief inspection of the ruined supermarket and liquor store, Maitland noticed with amusement that the beauty salon was still intact. The bank, with its barred-off area behind the teller's wickets, had at one time been converted into a kennel, with dog and cat travel cases stacked upon each other in the spacious safety deposit vault.

He poked his head into the recreation area. The stale air was faintly perfumed with chlorine, and a confusion of bones, shopping carts and wine bottles traced a strange pattern at the bottom of the drained swimming pool. The lift doors on this floor opened, but his torchlight revealed their use as a garbage disposal. A lightweight chain sealed the fire steps, and he quickly cut through it to reveal a clear passage up. By the time he got to the 20th floor he heard a faint, far-off, high-pitched howling — dogs on the hunt. Pausing briefly, Maitland threw a couple handfuls of his doctored biscuits on the steps a few floors below him. At the entrance to the 25th floor he met a major roadblock of stacked furniture.

By sheer luck he pulled on a chair leg — which proved to be the master lever that opened a hole just big enough for him to squeeze through. The dogs went quiet behind him. Past the barrier, he surveyed the lobby — now an art gallery of greasy polaroids taped and pinned to the walls. He got out his torch and took a closer look.

Most were jarred, motion blurred photos of people fighting, bloody faces, and drunken cheering, but many were of macabre scenes of dead people dressed in often surreal costumes with ornate face make-up, posed in various sexual positions. He turned away and splayed his light around. Desiccated bags of garbage lined the walls.

He noticed a slight draught playing on his face from the aisle to the right of the lift. Rounding the corner he heard a faint flapping sound, like a small bird struggling in the paws of a bored cat. He crept along to an open door and looked inside. The flat stretched out from the dull carpet under his shoes to the shining air outside. Straight ahead on the sitting room floor a notebook's pages chittered in the breeze from the open balcony door. He picked it up, took a quick glance, pocketed the book and instinctively closed the large sliding glass door. Maitland turned and quickly assessed the flat. It was in relatively good shape. He spent a few minutes looking through the bedroom, noticing there was a hole in the floor where a plank had been removed, and in the tiny kitchen he was somehow not that surprised to discover a bag of old letters, all addressed to the rather enigmatic Dr Laing. Richard was correct about the location. The morphine. Was any still here?

He returned to the living room to ponder his next move and while staring out the window he was startled by a loud sniffing sound from the hallway. He turned to see a smallish man dressed in a torn and stained Superman costume, with the furry remains of an Alsatian's head for a hat.

Letting out a low growl, Superman revealed a dentist's drill in his right hand and simultaneously lunged towards Maitland, who stood frozen on the spot and then casually kicked a small side table into Superman's charge. The rim caught the caped crusader on the shin, throwing him forward, arms flailing for balance as he made a final attempt at recovery before falling nose first into the balcony's glass door and bouncing backwards, dazed, to the floor. Blood seeped over his cheeks and into the headpiece.

Maitland gave him a tentative kick to the ribs and stepped over the body, out of the flat, down the hallway and into the service area where he could find Royal's lift door. He closed the door behind him, flicked the deadbolt, and waited for the lift to rise from the 10th floor. He got in and hit a button. At the 35th floor he stopped and made his way to the main lift lobby to find another empty swimming pool and the remains of a restaurant. He checked the stairwell going down — the landing was stacked with tables and chairs from the restaurant, and broken household furniture choked the steps down a whole floor. Apparently no one from the lower levels was going to be invited higher for dinner and a dip. Conversely, the steps up to the roof were clear.

Maitland checked his watch. It was nigh on noon and he sat down in the restaurant to review his immediate situation. Apparently, the high-rise was still occupied, if only by an inept madman in a kid's costume. And a few dogs, perhaps kept. And the unexplored building, already revealing itself to be generally divided into territorial areas. Classic tribalism, he realized. Tree forts. That thought took him back to his youth, when rather than play and fight with other kids, he preferred creeping through abandoned houses and derelict buildings. His explorations would keep him amused for hours, searching for the often-surreal remains and bits of prior occupants, prior lives. This building was forty floors of much more intriguing possibilities.

A faint bark from deep in the stairway snapped Maitland from his reverie. Time to reach the top. A few minutes later the lift's rooftop door appeared and he carefully opened it, blinking in the harsh sunlight. An unexpected flurry of large white birds briefly startled him as he rounded the lift head and walked onto the terrace. Did he also see a figure in white out of the corner of his eye? He paused. Stretching out on the roof in front of him was a large, white-tiled rectangle. Randomly placed on this grid was a collection of large, geometrically shaped objects mounted on pedestals. Off to the right were dozens of large plant pots, many with greenery, and to the left a glass-walled room went right to the edge of the roof. Maitland stepped forward, belatedly recognizing the geometric forms as sculptures, and wondered about the flowing discolourations that stained the spheres, pyramids, cubes and the white tiles underfoot — like Jackson Pollock had run amok with gallons of dark red paint. At the far end of the sculpture garden he noticed a large black burnt area, and on either side of it sat a strange apparition which seemed to resemble parts of a callisthetics machine, but was obviously reconfigured to be used as support for a large roasting spit.

Maitland looked into the glassy room — obviously Royal's office. Desk, table, sofa, chairs, filing cabinets — all undamaged. A clever glass door enabled entrance to the office area once inside he noticed a set of steps descending into the high-rise. He figured it went to the 40th floor's main lobby with its high-speed lifts. He crept down. All was silent. A double door entrance off the lobby was open and Maitland crept into a truly impressive flat. Then he noticed the walls were clean, the carpets unstained, and curtains hung peacefully around the high windows in the slightly musty living room. On the large dining room table stood two silver candlesticks. He returned to the flat's foyer and entered the lobby. It had no barricades, no garbage bags, and the expensive furniture was present and still intact. The walls had also been cleaned, although some faded graffiti still stubbornly remained. He opened the door to the emergency stairs and they appeared to stretch cleanly down a number of floors.

Returning to Royal's penthouse, Maitland began a systematic search of the rambling flat, which stretched half the length and the full width of the high-rise. In the library he found an unopened bottle of Italian wine — something red and strong from the Del Baldo estate — and by the time he had checked out all of Royal's home and explored the top three floors the late afternoon sun was beginning to smear the towers of London into an orange haze, and giving in to some unknown impulse he decided to spend the night.

He grabbed the candles and the sheets from a bed, and returned to Royal's rooftop aerie. A few large white gulls circled above, finally landing on the roof's outer wall and rubbing their beaks in red-stained concrete crevices. Back in the ostentatious office, he laid out the contents of his backpack on a draughting table.

The lazy twilight beckoned, and Maitland grabbed a chair and the wine and wandered out into the sculpture garden. The golden air lightened the dull red patina on the various works, one of which caught his eye: three cement ovoids, stacked vertically, each slightly smaller than the one beneath it. Damn modern art, he thought, munching the sandwiches he should have had for lunch. He took a swig from the wine bottle and for some reason again felt like a teenager out on an adventure. Could someone actually live here? He eyed the big birds appraisingly.

It was becoming cooler in the twilight and he tugged his jacket closer. There was something in the right pocket. He

Damn modern art, he thought...

retrieved the notebook he had found in Laing's flat on the 25th floor. It was about the size of a thin paperback novel, quite beat up, and had a stain on most of the back cover. Or was that blood?

He opened it. The first page was inscribed at the top with a neat LAING, with 2525 underneath. A quick flip of the few pages revealed it was some sort of diary, to-do reminders, recipes, and lists of names, many with a line drawn through them. He thumbed back to the beginning:

> Night. Girls asleep. Building still quiet. I'm sitting on the balcony pecking at the dog's overcooked leg when all the lights went off on the 7th floor of our sister high-rise. Could hear some of the shouts from here. Tomorrow need to set more traps.

> At one time all the dogs were on the top floors, and the children mostly below the 10th. Now it's reversed. None of the telephones work.

> Not sure of the date. Does it matter? Steele becoming more dangerous at night, altho being right beside him may be safest as he seems to be ranging wider, and he has a dog. Bait or food? Alice is becoming weaker. Eleanor is still demanding batteries. Time to increase the doses of M?

Maitland paused for a drink. Darkness was deepening so he decided to move indoors. With candles lit he snuggled down on the office sofa with the wine and Laing's notes. For a few pages there were just lists of names, as if Laing was keeping track of what must have been a dwindling population. Then he read …

> Rossi's Roast Rover: a spit set over a fire pit

with wood fuel is the ideal way to roast a whole dog. Can also be used for cat, raccoons, large whole poultry, or any other large pieces of meat. Trussing a whole or partial dog is very important. Then make one long slit down the back and several diagonal slits on each side. None of the slits should touch any other. Then rub the dog with any oil or fat you may have on all its surfaces. Begin cooking. Rotate the spit quickly enough to keep the juices from dropping. After about 30 minutes or so begin basting liberally with fat and any garlic you may have. Baste every 10 to 20 minutes and, when done, set the roast dog aside to rest for about 30 minutes. First remove the shoulder and hind-legs at the joints. These pieces then can be sliced to serve. Next make a cut down the middle of the back, down the spine. Then cut from the shoulder, hugging the bone of the ribs and spine, down to where the rump and hind-leg were removed. This large piece will include the rack and loin cuts as well as the dog's belly.

The next few pages were covered with what looked like a scratchy floor plan of the 25th floor, with various distances marked along hallways. Maitland laughed as he continued to read ...

Found it today! Was looking around the service lift area and finally discovered where my measurement anomaly was hidden — behind a stack of mattresses, a small steel door. It wasn't locked. Inside a stairway and a vertical shaft. It was easy to walk down to the basement, and there it was: a mini-lift. Room for two. Best: the lift's electric system was separate from the building and throwing a switch started it up. Royal was clever — big rubber wheels and the engine in the basement means the cage runs silently. Now we can escape from Steele, who has run out of bodies to dress up and has replaced his dead models with mannequins from the 10th floor's fashion shops. He's also found a storage of costumes from somewhere, which he either wears on his night raids or drapes over mannequins. He may also be training dogs on the lower floors. The protection he claims to be giving us is costing too much M.

Christ, they're all strung out, Maitland thought, then slightly chuckled as he finished off the Del Baldo. So Steele was his inept assailant, and Laing had figured it out and gained if not the territorial advantage, then certainly freedom of movement. His sense of control must have increased — but where was Laing now? Outside, the gulls had vanished with the night and on the horizon the lights of London glowed like an ersatz sunset through the dusty windows. He returned to Laing's notes ...

Weather warmer and much has changed over the past months. The lift has allowed me to improve our supply of food and water, and this has revived Alice and Eleanor ... they're now walking around a few hours each day and becoming more insistent in their demands ... and details of my excursions from the building.

Steele abandoned his home and moved to Wilder's on the second floor. He's claimed all the floors to the 25th and has chained the stairway higher. Aside from Steele's barricade on the first and 10th floors, the master block on the 25th and the huge wall at the 35th have been instrumental in keeping out strangers and separating the clans.

Maitland didn't recognize the names, but realized the barricades were still as described. The list of Laing's various observations went on and Maitland paused from the notebook. It was dark out. His silhouette threw enigmatic shadows on the walls of glass, and he was just about to blow out the candles and fade to sleep when he felt a slim hand at his throat and the oblique flash of a long carving knife.

Maitland raised his hands slightly. The notebook dropped. He whispered, "It's OK ... I'm a kind of architect. Just here for the night. If that's OK."

A woman in white cut into his vision. A face that had recently seen a mirror. Wavy blonde hair twisting over her shoulders. She appeared to be wearing something fashionable — a short skirt and finely finished silk blouse. Her breathing was calm as she warily circled the sofa.

"Who are you? Why are you here?"

"My name is Maitland. Robert Maitland. I'm a spatial psychologist and I'm interested in this building ... OK, I'm a kind of shrink who studies buildings. You can call me Bob. And you?"

"Anne. Anne Royal."

Maitland was surprised. "Tony's wife?"

"Ex-wife."

"Sorry. I knew Tony myself."

Her eyes narrowed slightly. "Unmissed. But he was the Royal Lord of this manor, and now I'm the Lady."

Maitland lowered his hands and bowed his head.

"Enchanted, m'lady."

Anne smiled slightly and sat behind Royal's desk. The knife disappeared. Two long legs appeared on the desktop.

Maitland flashed Anne his warmest smile.

"I'm sure we'll be the best of friends. Do you have any

here? Are you alone in the castle tower?" He pulled back the bedsheet and sat up on the sofa.

Anne looked out on the roof, now washed white in the moonlight. There was a faraway look in her dark eyes. "We had a sort of women's organization that lasted about nine months. Mums and kids, living and working together. Protecting each other. The eventual shortage of men — food — finally became a problem — yes, I know about Tony's lift — but there were too many of us and our original ideals began to fade — or evolve. Within two months I was the only sister left on the roof. The high-rise still contains quite a few people — there are secret and not-so-secret passages cut through floors and walls everywhere. But nobody above the 35th floor — this is mine."

"How do you survive?"

"You've already met my protection — Steele. He pretty well scares the shit out of anyone who wants to explore the high-rise or get past the big blockade at the 25th floor. How did you get past the dogs and wall? No matter. I keep him as the old school crazy, a reminder of our tribal time when it went instinctual. Nurses grudges. Is jealous of me. One of these days he … won't be necessary. Food? Protein is not very easy to find anymore. And cook. I'm growing veg in those pots on the roof, but water is bloody hard work to get up here, even with the lift. If I could only hook up a water pump — and I'm sure Tony had set up an alternate power source for the penthouse, but I can't find it — I'd have a little farm up here. This urban hunter-gatherer shit is OK for a while, but I'm willing to compromise."

Maitland wasn't so sure. He decided to change topics. "I'm also curious about one of the tenants here. A Dr Laing. Do you know him?"

Anne laughed. "We all know the Doctor, Robert — Bob. Hah — you both have the same first name. He was basically invisible and acquiescent during the, ahh … transformation, but then he emerged as a kind of cranky, bossy shopkeeper. Laing ran the drugstore. Traded drugs — morphine — for everything, but inevitably he ran out. Things got unfortunate then."

"Upset addicts?"

"Maybe, but it hit closer to home. Laing was quite pleased with his 'harem' — two fucked up women he controlled with drugs — who earned their keep by complaining. Don't ask. One of them, Eleanor, went missing, and soon after Laing's sister Alice died, possibly from withdrawal. Or an overdose. Laing hid her body."

"He did what?"

"Stashed it away somewhere — away from our psycho, Steele. He likes to take bodies and dress them up."

"I think I've already seen one. Anubis in the lobby."

"That's him, all right. Anyway, Laing didn't go long without a companion. A few weeks later Helen Wilder — who left the sisterhood — showed up at Laing's door with two kids and a broken cine camera. She wanted out and finally convinced him to clean up, put on a suit, and go back to the medical school. Last I heard Laing was back at his old job — they thought he's been on sabbatical in Africa, working on a water project in the desert. Hah. Maybe he was."

Anne suddenly froze. "Shhhh ..."

Then Maitland heard it — the faint howl of a beagle echoing up the building. Distant, but still too close. Could Superman really fly?

He looked at Anne. She didn't look happy, and motioned to Maitland to collect his stuff.

"That bloody Steele again. These little visits are becoming tiresome. Let's not have a confrontation."

Maitland refilled his knapsack, doused the candles, and both of them retreated to the wall behind the sculpture garden — he a dark shadow, she a shimmering flow of silver moonlight. They paused to wait. He liked the way she pressed up beside him. Presently the darting beam of a torch bounced up the white walls of the stairs and Steele, still in his Superman costume, slowly opened the door to the roof.

Four dogs rushed past his legs and began excitedly sniffing the ground. Not waiting for the dogs to catch their scent Maitland and Anne backed into the safety of the waiting lift. For some reason she stopped at the 25th floor.

Laing's flat was unchanged from this morning, save the fresh blood stains. Maitland made a rough barricade behind the door and flopped on Laing's large sofa. Anne stretched out beside him. He tried to review the day's events but the warmth of her body overcame him and soon he was in a deep sleep.

Maitland awoke in the early morning sun, unsure at first where he was. His back was stiff. Anne was in the kitchen. He still had food and a bottle of water left in his pack, but Anne had done a quick exploration of Laing's kitchen, finding various pots, broken dishes, a few mugs, and, surprisingly, a small jar still containing ground coffee. She poured some water into a pot and took it to the balcony, where a handful of telephone directory pages and some splintered chair legs soon made a small blaze in Laing's homemade fire pit, which looked suspiciously like a long metal meat tray from a butcher's shop. Coffee made, Maitland and Anne sat out on the balcony and basked in the early morning sun.

Maitland found himself straying from the view of London to Anne Royal. She was like someone from a desert island, an exotic, abandoned princess who probably went through men like Asian cooks used banana leaves.

He looked up to the penthouse high above. It seemed conceivable that power and water could be routed to the roof — he had the building plans — and he didn't think it would be too difficult to finally deal with Steele.

Anne smiled at him. Her face was golden.

Maybe, he thought, I could stay here a week or two...

Anne sat out on the balcony and basked in the early morning sun

LIGHT WAVES

It was around three in the morning when Steve was awakened by a loud, coarse cry. He opened his eyes. The cathedral ceiling of his bedroom was gone. It was damp. He realized he was not in bed but outside, lying on his back on grass he should have cut yesterday. All was still.

Above him, illuminated by the silver light of a near-full moon, a strutting bird walked the low branch of a towering fir tree. It stared directly at Steve. *Braawk, braawk*, it called out to nothing in particular. Stupid raven, Steve muttered, and as if in response it made a laughing sound and launched into the air, heavy wings beating noisily to the north over the Saanich Inlet. Steve thought that was odd.

Ravens don't fly at night.

He rolled over on one arm and looked around. His left shoulder was stiffer than usual. He grunted. The strangely bright moonlight illuminated his back yard — all seemed well — and then he noticed he was wet with dew. And in pajamas. He should have felt shocked, or at least curious about this unusual situation, but instead he felt a slight sense of *deja vu*, which also seemed inexplicable. Something about the moon? He tried to remember what he did last night … had he eaten something off? Licked a toad? Steve smiled at that one — where the hell would you find any toads here in Victoria, the boring capital city of super-natural British Columbia, Canada?

It was chilly. He grunted to his feet and wobbled across the sparkling lawn to his back deck and door. It wasn't locked. He made his way to the bedroom, changed pajamas, and slid into bed.

It was just past nine when he was roused from slumber by another audio intrusion. The doorbell. Why the hell did he buy one that sounded like Big Ben? He rolled out of bed, found a housecoat, and mumbled his way to the front door. Half expecting a couple of religious nuts with their brainwashed eyes, he was surprised to find a delivery van in his driveway and a guy standing on his porch with a tall cardboard box mounted on a dolly.

"Steven Trites?"

"Yup."

"Delivery. Can I get you to sign here?" He held out an ePOD.

Steve tapped the top of the box. "What's this?"

"I just deliver the packages, Mr. Trites … we don't look inside."

Smart ass. "I thought you might know where it came from. I didn't order anything."

"Says here a law firm in Vancouver."

"Dewey, Cheatem & Howe?" Steve loved that joke.

Unamused, the delivery man pointed to a small blank area on his electronic device. "Sign here, please."

Steve signed the screen the best he could and was happy the delivery man dollied the cargo into his foyer before leaving. An envelope was taped to the top of the imposing box, a cardboard tower big enough to hold a wine fridge. He ripped it off and trundled back to the kitchen. Laying the envelope on the table he busied himself with making coffee.

Java in hand, Steve sat and opened the envelope. It was from a law firm, all right, and explained the box was an inheritance from a distant clan of relatives he vaguely knew from stories he had heard as a youth. Fourth or fifth cousins to my grandmother, he remembered, as if that was a possible familial connection. Hell, he thought, we all must be distant cousins somewhere along the line.

Apparently, as the letter explained, the inheritance — whatever was in the heavy box — was a bit of a castaway. A long-forgotten relative had stored it for decades, died peacefully in her 90s, and left all to a great-grandchild a year ago. Nobody knew who originally owned it, nor did the inheritor want it, as he lived in Toronto and the box was in storage in Vancouver, so for a joke he opened an old family photo album, found a 1980s group shot of kids, and chose one of them. That lucky little tyke was Steve's father, who had recently died in a car crash, so the thing came to him. Congratulations.

Steve's brow furrowed. This all seemed ultra-fishy. Why go to all this time, trouble, and money when it could have simply been given to a thrift shop? Why not send someone in Vancouver to at least see what was in it? Steve eyed the box. Vertical rectangle. About three feet square, maybe five feet tall. Heavy. He got a paring knife from a drawer and the thin cardboard parted like his ex-wife to reveal a tall structure of intricately carved wood.

It looked like a trunk. He automatically squinted a bit. It was highly worked. He pulled away the rest of the cardboard and walked around it. The workmanship was definitely from somewhere in India, with decorated brass corners, huge hinges, and a big round lock … but the amazing parts were the side panels, each relief carved with the image of a bellowing elephant in profile, twisting in anger with one of its legs extended down to form one of the box's feet, while the uncurling elephant's trunk reached up to the top right corner, where the brass protector was decorated with images of what looked like tigers.

Great Ganesh's ghost, Steve thought, this is right out of *The Antiques Roadshow*. He eyed the lock. Too nice to forcibly open. No matter — it was unlocked. He wondered how long it had been since anyone had looked inside. Yes, how old was this thing, anyway? Certainly, it looked genuine, but he was no expert on Indian furniture. If it was actually old, it might be worth some money. It certainly was well carved, and on closer inspection he noticed each elephant had a bright carnelian eye.

The top flipped back smoothly on its hinges to reveal a layer of protective paper over the contents. A layer of fine dust indicated it had been untouched for a long time. A very long time. He folded the thick paper once, then across to keep the dust at bay, and put it aside. Inside were folded clothes. No treasure. He picked out two full tunics, pants, a great coat, two sets of boots, and two visor caps. They were Air Force uniforms. Old ones, too, like back to WW2. The markings revealed the owner was a Flight Lieutenant. Steve wasn't interested in old military stuff, but again he was drawn to their possible resale value. The cloth was in quite good shape — no moth ravages — and he knew there were many war memorabilia collectors keenly interested in uniforms, in themselves a high entropy item. And even more so for an officer's rank.

Then something unexpected. Just around three to four feet down Steve ran out of dry goods and hit a barrier. It was covered with the same flowery wallpaper as the sides, and when rapped it gave back a deep, thick response. No balsa wood here, Steve thought. He kept tapping and walked around the trunk's exterior. He could almost see where the blocking plank must be placed, leaving a gaping hole of mystery beneath it. He shook the now-lighter trunk. There was a faint movement in the hidden space.

Again, the choice: get out the drill and jigsaw and ruin the probably valuable trunk, or take a moment to think about it. What to do? His mind worked. Yes. There should be an access via a hidden toggle, or button, incorporated into the design. He looked at the trunk's panels again. There was a lot of design. He got on his hand and knees and ran his hands over the carved surfaces. Nothing. The brass corners didn't move. There were no hidden levers. The elephant eyes stayed fixed. He sat back, frustrated. What had he missed? Aha. Maybe a trap door on the bottom. He tipped the trunk over until it rested on the edge of a foyer chair. Not quite low enough. He grabbed one of the elephant feet to lower the trunk further and the foot moved in his hand. He looked at it. Another turn and a concealed panel popped open to the room.

Steve crawled around to get a better look at the cavity. The space was full. More clothes — T-shirts — all wrapped around something. More of the same? His enthusiasm rose when he grabbed the bundle of cloth and started to pull it out. There was something hard and heavy inside. Not what he was expecting, although he wasn't sure exactly what might have been hidden away by an air force pilot. He cautiously removed the package and carefully placed it on the kitchen table. It was quite easy to remove the cotton wrappings.

Before him was a circular, domed disc over two feet wide and a foot high at the center. The dome itself was made of 12 long wooden slats, each carved into a graceful curve, each painted a dark black and — he looked closer — each decorated with a curious pattern of mother-of-pearl chips that went from tip to base. The outline of a bird? The careful workmanship was obvious. He slowly rotated the object. Each slat was cleverly hinged to the side of an underlying mask, and each slat had a thin leather cord attached to its exterior — about two inches up — that ran down the slat and under the mask.

He gingerly opened the daisy face of strips to reveal another image underneath — a shiny white round face, surrounded with more esoteric insignias made of mother-of-pearl inlays. The opened slats were also white inside and carved like wing feathers. Steve tipped the mask up and looked underneath. The strands of leather met in a curious knot and then dangled free, and it was obvious this mechanism was designed to open the slats with a good pull. The carving itself was quite abstracted. It featured a short, hooked nose protruding from a circular, symmetric face, with big eyes, heavy brows, and an open mouth showing top and bottom teeth in an aggressive grimace.

Steve stared at the artifact. His thoughts about the value of the trunk and uniforms faded as the potential windfall this enigmatic mask represented dawned on him. He wished he had paid more attention to local Indigenous art. If this was old — over a hundred years — it might be worth tens of thousands. But he needed an expert opinion. Happily, he knew who to call — "Brother" Paul — an old client who had owned one of Victoria's largest indigenous arts stores, the ones so popular with wealthy Asian tourists. He found his phone and began taking a series of photos of the mask, closed, and opened, which he texted off to his old friend. Returning to the living room he cleaned up the chunks of cardboard, righted the trunk, and arranged the uniforms, boots, and hats in neat piles.

Again, he wondered — who was the original owner?

He was in the process of pouring another cup of coffee when the phone rang. It was Paul, the art dealer. He sounded excited.

"Steve… Stevie Trites… you old, retired rat… wassup? Long time, no see… pix arrived. What is that you've got? Looks like an old transformation mask. Impressive carvings."

"Not sure, Brother." He liked the level of interest in Paul's voice. "I just got it this morning — found it in an old trunk I apparently just inherited. Dunno much more about it."

"Old trunk? Whaddya mean, old trunk?"

Steve spent the next five minutes relating the events of the morning. Paul sounded a bit incredulous.

"Helluva story, Steve, what next will fall in your lap?"

Paul lowered his voice. "You gonna keep the mask? It's a beauty. Or maybe flog it? I can help you there — for a small commish — but I gotta warn you, sadly, if this mask is what I think it is you're going to be in a bit of a sticky problem, Steve-oh. This Indigenous stuff goes beyond art, and into the murk of culture. These artifacts were carted out by the boatloads — if I can mix transportations. Discoveries like this these days are going to need some strong proof of provenance to make them legal to sell." His voice dropped. "Unless you can find a very private collector who will keep the mask from being publicly known."

"I was hoping you might know a few of those guys."

"Well, yes, I still have some connections who might be interested. A lack of provenance doesn't matter that much in Shanghai."

"OK, Bro, cool. But I haven't even started to research the situation. First, the trunk belonged to some distant relative. There's a law firm involved. I can start with that. Then it should be easy to track his movements and hopefully discover where and when he bought or traded for this. Probably bought it. Basically, he lived and worked in the area so there should be some records."

"Good luck with that, Stevie. Discovering the history of this mask will make a big difference in the value. At least three zeroes worth."

Steve laughed. "OK, Bro."

"Tell you what I'll do — I'll forward these photos — nice, by the way — to a woman I know who teaches at the University of Victoria. She's a real expert in Indy art and I'm sure will be excited to see your mask. Expect a call from her — the name's Islay Buchanan. Pleasant academic."

"That's an oxymoron, but I'll await her call. If I find out

anything about this thing's history, I'll call you back, OK?"

"OK, adios."

Steve was pleased. Very pleased. He felt like he had discovered a horde of coins buried in his back yard. Back in the foyer he stacked the old uniforms and put them in the garage.

The trunk. What to do with it? He decided to drag it into the main floor guest bedroom. He'd figure out what to do with it after the mask situation clarified. Hold on, he realized, the trick door to the hidden compartment was still open. He reached around to close it and his fingers struck … paper. He looked inside. One sheet was at the entrance, and more stuck in the back. He pulled them out, took a quick glance at the first page, whistled an exhalation, went into his study, and sat at his desk. He spread the papers out in front of him.

Four were hand-written foolscaps, and the rest of the haul included several official-looking documents, and a photocopy of an honourable discharge from the Royal Canadian Air Force. Steve chuckled to himself … the missing provenance … he scanned down the page.

Name: Jamie Graham.

Birth: 15 November 1923.

Birthplace: Moose Jaw, Saskatchewan.

Enlisted: 4 July 1943.

Date of Discharge: 19 April 1946.

OK, Steve thought. Gotcha, baby. The rest of the papers revealed Jamie was a pilot, had spent his time at RCAF base Comox, halfway up the eastern coast of Vancouver Island, and he made regular C-47 Dakota runs to a range of radar stations situated on the Pacific side of the island. There was no mention of his address at discharge. Well, it was unlikely the house still be there anyway — everything had changed dramatically in 80 years. But he had a full name. Part of a history. A start. Then he read Jamie's rather breathless story.

Hello. My name is Jamie Graham, and I have a confession to make. I know what happened at Tofino. I've told no one about those events, nor have I revealed the existence of the artifact. Here's what I remember. It was on October 20, 1945, a Saturday — ten years ago as I write this — when I received orders to take a loaded Dakota C-47 from RCAF Comox to the airbase at Tofino and return the next morning with some of the technical crew from the radar station. I was bringing in food and fuel and should have taken off at 14:00 but was delayed to 18:00 with an engine problem. Didn't matter much, as the flight was roughly 20 minutes and the sun wouldn't dip into the Pacific until 18:50. Besides, there was a full moon and clear skies forecast.

The flight was easy, and my co-pilot Max and I landed at Tofino at 18:31 under cloudless cover in a brilliantly orange late twilight. The cargo, as usual, was unloaded onto a truck destined to risk the barely-built dirt road to the radar base the next morning. Max and I checked in at the control tower and discovered half the guys at the radar base were already in Tofino at the only bar, celebrating the health of the lucky guys heading back to civilization. Max decided to join them, but I'd seen those radar boys in action and didn't feel like drinking all night and getting stupid over fishermen's daughters. I grabbed a Jeep and headed south to the radar base.

I'm not much of a romantic, but the bumpy ride down the coast that night was like out of a Hollywood movie. All it needed was soppy music. And a curvy dame beside me. The full moon was up to around 10 o'clock in the sky, the tide was out, and the Pacific flowed in a sparkling crescendo as the surf uncurled on the dark, undulating sand. Even the barking of distant sea lions seemed softened by the light. It was magical for a prairie boy from Moose Jaw.

Soon enough I reached the base and, gearing down, turned up the steep service road to the general grounds. I reached the mess hall, parked, and entered to find the boys sitting around, some reading, but most playing a game of cards around a big table. It looked boring. It was. I'd never really warmed to these technical types. Flyboys like me were generally ignored, unless someone wanted a little something extra flown in, incognito style.

I wandered into the mess kitchen, poured myself a cup of coffee and went out into the general parking lot for a smoke. The night was surprisingly warm for a late October night, and the sky particularly clear. The stars hung like echoes of infinity. The full moon was so bright I could have read a newspaper. Light without colour.

A line of Douglas firs blocked the view out over the ocean, so I decided to drive up to the radar array and look out into the universe from there. The three radar rectangles sat precariously over a set of squat buildings on about an acre of land, looking like silver spider webs against the dark sky. The biggest receiver was front and centre, scanning west, and the other two smaller units pointed north- and south-west. The boys had built a long bench along the front of the complex, and I was just getting out of the Jeep to sit on it when I heard a very loud, strange, yet oddly familiar sound from the base beneath me. *Brrrawwwk. Brrrawwwk. Awwk. Awwk.*

I buzzed over to the cliff edge and looked down. The barracks, mess, parking lot and distant generator complex were brilliantly revealed in moonlight, and yet I couldn't see anything responsible for the noise. Then, off to the right, something dark emerged from the tree shadows. A hungry bear? Maybe, but there was an odd blob where the head should be. I squinted. There seemed to be something shiny, twinkling in the blob itself. My first thought was Hallowe'en — it was coming up soon. Maybe one of the boys was up to a prank with me. They knew I was coming. The squawking noise continued.

A few guys came out of the mess hall to see what was up — I could hear one of them call inside to the rest of the crew — and in a minute all were grouped around the front door. Somebody's arm reached out, pointing. I looked back to the dark figure and it, too, revealed arms that were moving up and down. The strange raven-like calls stopped, and the base crew began to move towards the apparition. I noticed one of the guys had a nickel-plated handgun that shone in the moonlight.

The dark figure stopped the arm waving and started wobbling whatever was above its shoulders. Then the arms reached up under what might be its chin. The arms yanked down, and the dark blob expanded to a large white concave circle, like someone fanning out a deck of cards. The men stopped. The white cone tilted up at the moon and, no lie, it started to glow more brightly, like it was intensifying the light. Its surface glow increased, pulsing in waves to an almost powder blue.

The creature then lowered its gaze towards the men, and swear to God, the ray of light that flowed from the cone turned into a slow pulsation, white to blue, white to blue, that engulfed the men and the ground in front of them like a strobing searchlight. Then it started.

The parking lot began to buckle and show signs of movement, which increased in strength and interval. It was liquifying! Immediately the men started to sink into the ground like it was quicksand, and just as the last man sunk beneath the churning dirt he took a shot in the direction of the intruder, who twisted around, grasping his left arm. The beam of light hit the ground in front of the thing and immediately melted it. The figure fell. The white thing winked out, and I unconsciously waved at a man's face just before it disappeared into the bubbling soil. I swear the face was laughing at me as it went under.

All went quiet. The moon was unperturbed. The lights still shone in the mess hall. Even the sea lions had gone quiet. I drove back down the service road and gingerly made my way onto the parking lot. It looked normal. I tested the ground before I walked over to where the bear-thing disappeared. Sitting on the now-solid ground was a black and white blob, splayed out, which I could now see was some kind of carved head gear. I picked it up. It was quite warm and made of wood. What to do?

I went back into the mess hall and sat down. I flopped the headdress on the table and returned the white blobs — they looked like flower petals — to their closed shape. The undersides had what looked to be a raven's head.

Being alone was unnerving and I couldn't stop wondering ... what the heck just happened? After about 15 minutes my mind settled down and I pondered my choices. It appeared on the surface I had basically just two: tell the story as I had witnessed it, and be yoked with the albatross of nuttiness, or simply say I had arrived at the base, and no one was around. I chose to play innocent and, to cover my tracks, wrapped up what must be an Indian headdress before returning to my Jeep and heading back to Tofino.

I told the base commander, who was predictably drunk, that I had gone to the hill to find it deserted. Lights on, nobody home. He laughed and said they knew I was arriving and probably pulled a joke on me. I agreed, and said I was going to sleep in the Dakota that night. I stashed the wooden mask in the plane's tail. Early the next morning my passengers, all hung over, and Max, even more hung over, arrived and we flew back to base at Comox.

Turns out the radar base commander couldn't find his men either, and a full investigation was called. My only participation was to testify about finding the base deserted. Well, what could they have thought my involvement was? I had no motive, and the base was pristine.

The military did their usual in explaining the loss of personnel, first calling them deserters, then looking accusingly at the local Clayoquot tribe, who were generally unfriendly, and finally going so far as to say the boys had been captured by a crew from a Japanese submarine. Nothing was decided, and so it ended. A few months later I was discharged from service. There's no history of this incident, except for this story and, of course, the headpiece. Do with it what you will — I've considered burning it."

Still thinking the story was just an elaborate hoax — maybe an invented yarn to cover up how he found or stole the mask — Steve decided to follow a hunch and do a search on the areas Jamie mentioned in his story. RCAF Comox opened its airfield in 1942 and by 1944 it was a centre for local air transportation. By 1946 the base was shut down and was reactivated in 1952. It was still operational. Straightforward stuff.

Tofino and its airport were just north of one of 10 radar bases hastily contructed in 1942 following the Japanese attack at Pearl Harbour — each specifically situated so there were no gaps in any coverage towards Japan. Located about five miles south of the small fishing village of Tofino, about halfway up the western coast of Vancouver Island, the base was situated on a high hill that rose abruptly from the beach.

Near the top a long, natural plateau housed the barracks, mess hall, radar control room and parking lot at one end, and opposite were the power generators and fuel tanks. A steep set of stairs went directly from the control room up to the hilltop — about 200 feet higher — which was home to a large radar unit and two smaller radar sets at the corners. An access road ran around the hill to the back of the radar towers. The installation was mothballed in the months after the Japanese surrendered in September, 1945. There were no mentions of personnel gone missing.

Steve looked again at Jamie's manuscript. Supernatural malarkey. It's just a mask. He gathered the papers together, stuffed them in an envelope, and locked them away in his filing cabinet.

He checked his watch. Already one pm. He felt a faint growl in his guts and wandered into the kitchen to make lunch. He cobbled together a sandwich and wandered out on the deck to eat and survey his yard.

The indented shape of his supine body was still apparent in the grass beside him. He had no idea how he ended up sleeping there. He was, in fact, having a difficult time even remembering what he did yesterday. His horror of dementia made a brief pass at the back of his mind. Couldn't be that, he thought, but what? Sleepwalking? As a youth he had been known to wander on occasion while in the land of Nod, but that was long ago. Quite long ago. Still, there were few other options to explain away his midnight ramble to oblivion.

His thoughts moved on to the events since waking on the lawn — surely a diary entry feast of all that's fantastic. The unlikely reason he received the inheritance. The trunk. The uniforms. The mask. And the crazy story. What next?

His telephone played the opening riff to *Whole Lotta Love*. "Steve speaking."

"Dr. Trites?" It was a female voice.

"Yes, you got him. Hello."

"Hi, Steve. I'm Islay Buchanan from the University of Victoria. I specialize in west coast Indigenous art and mythology, and I've been looking at some mask photos of yours Paul sent to me."

"Hi, thanks for the call. That was fast. Paul said he was sending those shots to you. Whaddya think?"

"I think you've either got something very special, or something not so special some carver knocked off for a quick sale. It looks good, but I can't tell. I'd like to make a closer examination."

"Sure, easy peasy. You want I should bring it to you, or you could come here? Fine either way. I am out of town, though ... Willis Point."

"Paul said you were out in the sticks. I'm at the University now but have an appointment in Brentwood Bay in a couple hours ... that's close to you ... should be finished around seven ... I could drive to you then ... probably show up around seven-thirty. Would that be acceptable?"

"Sure, fine. I've got one of those backlit house number signs out front. The address is 3399 Lawrence Lane and be careful, it's a tight right-hand turn into the driveway. See you then."

"OK, bye."

Steve turned off the phone and gave himself a big smile in the reflecting kitchen window. He moved the mask onto the dining room table, covered it with a towel, made an early dinner, cleaned up, enjoyed the sunset with a glass of wine, and awaited his guest.

It was just around 7:30 when Steve heard the crunch of car tires on the long gravel driveway, and he grandly opened the front door to his guest just as she was about to hit the doorbell.

"Greetings, Dr Buchanan. Right on time! C'mon into my humble hacienda."

"Thanks, Steve. Please call me Islay."

"Happy to. Let's go to the living room. Would you like a drink? Wine? Water? Coffee?"

"Glass of white would be pleasant ... but not too much. That's one wiggly road to get in and out of here."

"Reduces the traffic to locals."

Steve led her along a hallway and down a few stairs to the living room and its dramatic outlook over the picturesque Saanich inlet.

"Make yourself comfy... I'll grab us some vino."

He returned with two chilled glasses to find Islay standing on the back deck, taking in the view. Giant firs and shiny arbutus trees lined his substantial lot, and the grassy yard was divided into several stone-walled platforms cascading down to the dark, calm water. A full moon was just rising over the distant Malahat Ridge.

"Gorgeous place, Steve ... or as Paul calls you, The Doctor. Cheers." They clinked glasses. "Medical or academic?"

"Hah ... that bloody Paul. It's neither, Islay ... The Doctor is a nickname I picked up in my late 20s when I found myself in a bloody horde of people trying to buy tickets to some rock show. Everyone was jostling around when some guy starts yelling from behind me, 'Excuse me, I'm a doctor ... excuse me ...' and everybody parts to let this guy through. I figure snap! — whatta great idea. After that every time I found myself in a crowd or lineup, I would just raise my right arm, wave my hand a bit and call out ... 'I'm a doctor ... excuse me' and the seas would part. I just became ... The Doc."

"Fascinating."

Steve just caught her incredulous sidelong glance as she turned from the view. She raised her glass again. "Well, Doc, let's unmask your mask."

"It's right here." Steve led her into the dining room and, true to his campaign presentation instincts, waited a few moments for her to focus her attention before removing the towel.

She couldn't help uttering a tiny, "Oh."

She reached out and pulled back the black slats. "Oh."

Her demeanor changed. She reached into her jacket pocket and brought out a pair of glasses and her phone. Glasses on, she tapped her phone a few times, bent over for a closer look, and started quietly dictating into the device. After many minutes of what seemed like incoherent mumbling to Steve she straightened up and took a few photos of her own.

"Amazing, Steve, simply amazing. I'd date this to around 1885 and I think I know the carver, a famous Haida chief known as Idansuu, who was basically known for his incredible totem poles and highly fluid argillite carvings. But he never made masks. I think this is his carving, so this may be the only mask he ever made." Her voice dropped. "Amazing."

"Is it valuable?" Steve sounded hopeful.

She gave him the look that said cultural leper. "This is an incredible piece of native art, Steve, and yes, it is valuable. If I'm right, it's verging on priceless. OK, high six figures. How did you get it again? Paul said you found it in a trunk. Really?"

"I did … an inheritance from some remote relative. I know his name, though. And he found it in Tofino in 1945." Steve had decided not to share Jamie's story with her — why look like an idiot?

"Tofino … that's odd. One would certainly have expected something this important to the Haida tribe would have stayed on their home island, Haida Gwaii. Probably stolen by a priest. Or archeologist. Or, it might have been a potlatch gift to a chief of the Clayoquot. They had a big settlement near Tofino. Do you know any more?"

"Sorry. Working on it. Are you going to tell me what it is?"

"Surely … what you have is a transformation mask. This

is a moon mask, part of the story of how the Raven tricked the Sky Chief, stole light from him, and gave it to humans. When Raven grabbed the light and flew away to make the sun a bit of light fell off, which became the moon." Islay closed the slats over the white face. "The Haida knew a lot about the moon, its influence over the tides, and even that moonlight is slightly polarized. Notice there are 12 black slats, representing the New Moon, which happens only once in a month. Also notice the design in mother-of-pearl and what looks like argillite … it's a stylized raven with outspread wings and the moon in his beak. See how carefully Idansuu was able to disguise the eyeholes in the overall design."

Steve was somewhat startled when she firmly grasped the top of the mask and gave a pull to the leather cords that curled out from the bottom. The slats silently flipped open.

"One pull and the dancer transforms from New Moon to Full Moon." She pointed to the design on the white slats. "See these? They look like feathers, but they're actually waves, emanating out from our guy in the middle here, who is in reality the raven turned human. The metaphoric transformation is dark to light, raven to man, and that flip gives the wearer access to the full moon's supernatural powers, which is tidal control over any liquids."

She put away her phone and glasses.

"What I find very unusual — perhaps unique — is the masculine face … it's basically always feminine — a noblewoman with a small ornament in her lower lip. The image is also strongly aggressive, another oddity. Too early to tell now, but this mask may have been made by Idansuu for a very specific purpose … don't know what yet. To use an indigenous Coast Salish term, this is a *skookum* mask, Steve. Powerful."

"I'm liking what I'm hearing," Steve said. "This is very very exciting news."

She gave Steve a wan smile and finished her now-warm

glass of Chardonnay. "For a lot of us." She looked at her watch.

"Oh, jeez … look at the time. I have an early class tomorrow … gotta run." She rifled through her pockets and handed Steve a business card.

"Here are my numbers. I'm sure we'll be in touch soon. You've got an amazing mask here, Steve … an historical find of high importance."

Steve watched Islay's taillights twist away up the driveway. He scowled. She was certainly going to report the discovery of the mask to her colleagues. Word will spread. The Haida will be notified. Government agencies will take notice. That cunning Paul, he thought, he's setting me up to sell it secretly for the juicy commission rather than give it back. Greedy bastard. He went back into his study and unlocked the filing cabinet. Had he missed something in Jamie's story? He was most curious about the tidal control powers Islay had suggested the mask influenced.

Again, the story was inconclusive … he only said he saw the earth move, then buckle, but he was 200 feet away and even with the full moon his vision must have been compromised somewhat.

Jamie — where had he got his hands on the mask? His story, his improbable story, started to sound like a cover to hide something more sinister. His research had found no records of anyone missing at this location in 1945. He also wondered if chatty Dr. Islay might be wrong and it's just a nice artifact instead of being carved by that old Haida Chief.

He looked again at the manuscript and this time noticed the date: 20 October 1945. He glanced the calendar on his computer. Today was also 20 October, but 80 years later, and the moon was also full. And bright enough to illuminate the soffit under the skylight in his study. An idea began to form.

He finished his wine, put the Jamie papers away, and

went into his closet where he undressed and put on some black pajamas. They do make me look thinner, he thought. He went into the dining room and gingerly lifted the mask off the table. It felt different — a little heavier — and when he walked it into the living room the decorations on the dark slats seemed to twinkle, but not in a way he could directly see — more from the corner of his eye. Steve wondered if it was a symptom of his recent intraocular lens implants.

Outside, he walked past the deck and onto his immediate lawn, where he had awoken early that morning. A light dew dampened his feet, and he looked up at the full face of the moon as it drifted across the north sky. Its reflection danced off the water. The man in the moon looked down with his unchanging, bored expression. The thought suddenly occurred he knew a guy who couldn't see any face at all in the full moon. Pareidolia-phobic, Steve thought.

It was time. He held the mask upright in front of him, slats facing in, New Moon style. He found the knot for the 12 cords that hung down, checked around to see he was alone, took a breath, and raised the mask to his face.

All went black.

His first, pulse-increasing sensation was one of being physically sucked into the mask as it molded itself around his face, then an odd flash. He squinted through the mask's eye slits. Moonlight flooded the area. He didn't recognize his surroundings, but it all seemed oddly recognizable. He was near the end of a field of sorts, with some low, light-filled buildings at the end. There was a rocky cliff to his left and a line of trees obscured the view to his right. In the moonlight he could make out a couple shapes moving in the far-off building.

"Hey, hello … hey!" Steve called out, walking slowly towards them. A couple men, curious, came out of the building.

Steve walked closer and called out again. "Hi, hello,

where am I?" The men turned and called into the building behind them. Soon a small crowd had formed.

At first Steve thought the mask, tight to his head, might be affecting his speaking. He was calling out in English but what he was hearing sounded more like the raucous caws from his local crows and ravens. He reached up to rub his throat and his hand touched the dangling leather cords. He instinctively pulled down hard and the mask opened. The full moon was just above the tree line over the barracks-like buildings. He looked at it.

The concave shape of the slats immediately collected the moonlight and broadcast it forward in a loose cone of shimmering white light. The group of men were instantly illuminated. A few of them raised their hands to shield their eyes from the brightness. The light intensified and began to pulse. The group started walking towards him. Someone called out. Steve noticed one of the men had a something in his hand, glinting like danger.

"Hello, hello! I'm lost. I need help!" His voice still didn't work. He tried to raise his arms over his head to signal submission, but the extended slats of the mask got in the way. He tried to pull off the mask. It wouldn't budge. He heard some shouts from the crowd in front of him.

The light from his mask had started to pulse with a blue tinge, and the gravel from his feet to the group leader began shaking, then rolling. Waves started to appear in front of him and the ground started to buckle as the intensity increased. Wherever he looked the ground started to liquify and he watched with helpless shock as the men before him cried out and began to quickly disappear into the fluid ground. There was a flash just as the last man went under, and Steve twisted to the left and doubled over slightly as a bullet ripped through his shoulder.

The mask was pointing at his feet.

As the ground bubbled up around him and Steve felt

himself slipping into it, he laughed with realization. Finally, the mask fell off. Before being swallowed by the blackness he looked up the hill and, in the moonlight, saw a man standing at the cliff edge, staring down at him. Waving.

He laughed once and all went black.

It was around three in the morning when Steve was awakened by a loud, coarse cry. He opened his eyes. The cathedral ceiling of his bedroom was gone. It was damp. He realized he was not in bed but outside, lying on his back on grass he should have cut yesterday. All was still.

Above him, illuminated by the silver light of a near-full moon, a strutting bird walked the low branch of a towering fir tree. It stared directly at Steve. *Braawk, braawk*, it called out to nothing in particular. Stupid raven, Steve muttered, and as if in response it made a laughing sound and launched into the air, heavy wings beating noisily to the north over the Saanich Inlet. Steve thought that was odd.

Ravens don't fly at night.

JACKSON WHOLE

I was reading a marketing trade magazine in the offices of the Frog & Duck, Advertising Messages Ltd. It was a Friday, just around noon. I had my feet up and outside the Vancouver sun was shining. It was July 3rd. Tomorrow was my birthday.

I was reading a story about F&D. Yes, it felt strange to be reading about yourself. The article was in a Toronto trade magazine by a Toronto writer, exclaiming about how F&D was a good example of Vancouver's trendy new move to "bizarre" agency names.

Truth was, a lot of us guys were finding ourselves on the street, so we had little choice but to start up creative boutiques, as they were called, small shops that didn't take on the financial risk of media buys, but simply specialized in dreaming up variations on the outrageous or humourous, mostly to attract the gullible to mass-volume retail clients. The article contained a pix of The Frog looking creative in his office. Jay-G, our financier, was never mentioned.

The phone rang. I was slightly peeved at this interruption. Friday afternoon to Vancouver is, you must remember, as the 7th day is to God. A time to get laid back and reminisce about the peaks or pratfalls of the preceding week. In other words, a time to hang out at the regular watering hole and lie about business to your ad game drinking buddies.

The phone rang twice. Cleveland picked it up. She cheerfully announced "Effen-Dee" and then lapsed into attentive silence. She smiled, wrote something down and called out to me. I looked up. "Line three. It's The Frog." I picked up the phone. Froggie sounded slightly testy. "Get over here right away, OK? The Ollie Jay-G's got something important to tell you." He hung up. I hung up, got up, put on my suit jacket, grabbed my cigs and headed out. I pushed through the old train station's immense front doors and hit Water Street.

I headed east, ducked down an alley in Gastown and entered The Restaurant. Ingrid the hostess recognized me and pointed off to the far corner. The Frog and Jay-G were hunched over a stack of dirty plates and two large glasses of wine. I sat down between them. He and Jay-G seemed to be involved in some kind of staring contest.

Ingrid brought me a clean wine glass. Frog finally looked away. Jay-G's eyes were looking wild. It took him about a minute to calm down. The sign came when he reached in his coat for a cigar.

Frog turned to me and said, "Ollie Duck, this is not easy. Jay-G has some news that, *malheusement*, is not going to be your favorite."

I looked across the table at Jay-G. He was leaning forward, trademark stogie clamped between two oversized fingers. His nails had been buffed shiny. His face appeared earnest.

"Duck, old boy, as the Frog has already blurted out, I'm afraid I have some bad news for you. For all of us. Beane has gone over the books, and things don't look so good.

"Cut to the chase," Frog said.

Jay-G nodded. "Frog & Duck is fucked. Kaputsky. Gone down the drain." He fingered his wine glass. He took a quick drink and looked straight at Frog. His voice was toneless.

"I got no choice. As majority shareholder and co-signer

of the note, I'm declaring Frog & Duck bankrupt. Operations will cease today. Duckie, you can clean out your desk this afternoon. Frogger, you and I will talk later."

The blood drained from my cheeks. I was glad I hadn't eaten. This was fucking great timing. Just a year earlier I had lost my own small shop, Duck Advertising Devices (DAD), when three of my four clients had hit the skids. Times were tough. Frog had started up his first shop two years ago, starting off with a paramilitary campaign to advertise his new agency. The campaign theme was *Frog Leaps Into Combat* and it featured Frog in a World War Two pilot's leather helmet. His credentials were prominent in bomb explosions across the bottom of the ad. Frog and I had talked a few times at bars. When DAD folded Frog took me in as a junior partner and we changed the name to F&D. Now it looked like I'd have to start all over again.

"Fuckin hell," I said.

"A bottle of Glen and three shot glasses," Jay-G called out to Ingrid. When the booze arrived, Frog filled the three glasses and carefully put one in front of each of us. He lifted his glass towards Jay-G.

"We gave it a good try, but we came up short. That's the way it goes sometimes. But before we hit the handle for the final flush I'd like to say something. Jay-G, I'd like to thank you personally for extending your credit as long as you did, and I also want to thank you for being a great partner and a great Ollie all together." We drank. Then nobody said anything for about five minutes. It was a long time.

Jay-G turned to me and said real slow. "Duckie, I'm going to write you one hell of a letter of recommendation."

The Frog started to tremble beside me.

Jay-G started to snicker. He leaned over the table and patted me on the cheek.

"Gotcha! Ducko. Christ, man, we toasted you. You're whiter'n cocaine." He laughed. Frog laughed. Ingrid laughed from behind the bar. "Duckie, ha ha." I was getting pissed off. I pouted.

"Chill out," Jay-G said smoothly. "The agency's doing just great. We're makin money." He laughed again at me, looked up, raised his hand and snapped his fingers.

"Ingrid, *l'edition*."

I looked at both of them.

"Assholes," I said.

"Happy birthday, Duckman," Frog said, raising his glass. "It's good to have you with us."

"Yeah," Jay-G raised his glass, too. "How old will you be tomorrow, anyway?"

"Thirty," I said. They looked at me suspiciously.

We drank one more shot of scotch. Then Ingrid arrived with the check. "Ingrid, my Swedish delight," he said, "bring us a phone, darlin." Ingrid curtseyed.

"You know what I want to do, Frog," Jay-G said. "I want to go out for dinner. A birthday dinner for The Duck." He knocked back his shot and looked around the restaurant. It was almost empty. "And I want to hear a little country & western music, too." He started singing a Willie Nelson song. It sounded final.

The phone arrived. Frog called Cleveland and asked her if everything was set up. He nodded yes to Jay-G and put the phone down. Jay-G passed the phone over to me. "Here, call your old lady and tell her you're going out for dinner tonight." He looked at Frog. "Whaddya think," he said "Calgary or Jackson Hole?"

I dialed home. She was in. I told her what was happening. She wished me well. I hung up.

"Let's go," Jay-G said. "If we're going country & western, we gotta dress the part."

We waltzed out of the restaurant, sashayed up the alley to the street, and turned south two blocks to The Western Shop, one of F&D's smaller clients. Inside we got down to it.

Billyboy, Jay-G's self-styled bodyguard, was already there and dressed in denim. They closed the shop's doors and we all picked out our own versions of what I chose: new Tony Lama boots, new jeans, a Budweiser belt with a bottle opener on the reverse of the buckle, a brand new hat, and best of all, a red western shirt with hundreds of white pearl buttons, white piping, and a royal flush in hearts spread out over each shoulder. We checked each other out, laughed, and hit the sidewalk. At the curb was a big limo. The four of us got in. The driver had cold beer waiting.

At the airport we turned left and headed out to the executive airpark. Jay-G's Lear was warmed and ready. We climbed in and took off. At about 35,000 feet over Washington state I figured Calgary was not on the menu.

We amused ourselves with a little gambling, but as no one ever intended to pay the other, the game didn't have much of an edge. Frog soon settled in to looking out the window and doing some serious damage to our stock of beer. After a couple hours the co-pilot leaned back and yelled to us we were starting our descent. We looked out the windows as the plane banked into a long clean glide and landed in the late twilight. We got out, stretched, and walked right into the arms of a US Customs Official. Frog was pretty drunk. Jay-G talked with the customs officer briefly, then the officer walked over to us.

He asked the usual. We all nodded yes. "OK, go," he said. We said good night to the pilots and climbed into a big Dodge van.

"This is the biggest taxi they've got," Billyboy said to no one in particular.

"Where to, sir," the taxi driver asked.

"The Million Dollar Cowboy Bar," Jay-G said. "And step on it." The gravel flew.

We arrived at the bar. It was huge. It was divided into two large rooms: a regular bar at the front and in the back, cowboys and cowgirls were whoopin it up in the dancehall. We looked around. The people in the bar looked at us. We looked overly well-dressed. OK, stupidly drugstore cowboy overdressed. Jay-G sidled up to the bar. We all followed. I was amused to see that instead of bar stools with seats, the Million Dollar Cowboy Bar had stools with real saddles on top.

Everyone crowded around Jay-G. I climbed up on a saddle and ordered a drink.

Billyboy was beside me. He ordered a big tray of shooters. The bartender didn't even look up. I got out of the saddle and watched. Billyboy grabbed the tray and made a beeline to the pool tables and started passing out free drinks. He didn't get beat up. They thought it was great. We joined in.

I took my drink and wandered back into the dance hall area to check out the action. A band, sorta country, was banging out a horn-heavy version of *Ghost Riders In The Sky* to an appreciate audience. A skinny little Yank wearing beatup boots, cheap jeans and a Houston Texans T-shirt came up to me and offered to trade his shirt for mine. He looked like a real cowboy. Did he think I was nuts? Billyboy appeared with a fresh tray of shooters. We both downed one.

At the bar, Frog was drunkenly trying to arrange dinner. It was getting late. I was feeling a little light-headed from the booze and lack of food, so I wandered out onto the street. We were right across from the town park. I crossed the street.

Over the park entrance rose a gothic arch of meshed deer antlers. Thousands of them, locked together like a million knobby fingers. I walked through the Park until the chill air revived me, then walked back to the bar. When I arrived Jay-G and Billyboy were involved in an animated discussion with a uniformed guy beside a white and black station wagon. In the back of the wagon a German shepherd was in a frenzy of barking. Billyboy finally pulled Jay-G away. We crossed the street and got in the cab. Jay-G was pissed.

"Where we goin?" he asked hoarsely.

"The best steak joint in town," Frog answered. "Thick as you like."

"All right," we all answered. It was nearly ten o'clock. I was starving. We drove for a few minutes and pulled up in front of an old-fashioned cafe. I looked in through the window. Tile floor. Red & white checked tablecloths. Old school.

We were just about ready to order when the cops arrived. The local police weren't too happy about Jay-G taunting their precious mutt, so we were being asked to leave. Actually, we were being told to leave. One of the cops went back to his car. Jay-G followed. I looked in at the selection of home-baked pies in the counter display. A few minutes later Jay-G returned.

"The pilots are on their way back to the plane. They're opening the airport."

We all piled in the Lear, hung over, hungry, and sloshing each other with the extra beer we bought with us. We arrived in Vancouver as pre-dawn lit the horizon. The customs man was there. He looked at us and laughed. We were still wearing our new duds, wet and smelly with beer. There were two limos. Jay-G jumped in one and sped off. The rest of us piled into the other and we were off. Two miles later our chauffeur was pulled over for speeding.

I arrived home at six. I stood at the end of the bed, tall in my new boots. She awoke and looked at me. Five minutes later she was still laughing. I wore the cowboy outfit to four Halloween parties before I outgrew the shirt. The toe of one boot cracked open three years later. The hat was destroyed in a street snowball fight the night before a Grey Cup game in Edmonton. I never wore the belt again. The jeans are these cutoffs I'm wearing right now. Refresh your drink? Dip in the pool? Didja hear about Jay-G's trip to Papua, New Guinea?

WHITE OUT

Warren awoke to a dizzy room. Or was it just his head spinning? A hit of vertigo? He realized he was lying almost sideways on his bed, head over the edge, pillow on the floor. When his vision stabilized, he noticed the pictures on his wall were askew. He got up, stumbled slightly navigating the end of his bed, and reached out for the dark curtains, pulling them open with his usual dramatic flair to bask in the unchanging glorious view of the verdant valley and placid river below.

It was all white out.

Large white fluff balls calmly filled and floated in the air, occasionally refracting a metallic sheen. Some flakes appeared to be settling, but the majority seemed happy to float along horizontally, dipping and twisting in what must be a wind, although Warren couldn't remember ever feeling any wind outside his house before.

Whiteness had already covered the back yard to what he thought was a couple feet, a guess because the fluttering dance of flakes made the surface slightly out of focus. It was white as far as he could see. A few cars and the occasional lorry still cautiously travelled the valley road, but nothing else moved save the flakes.

Warren squinted slightly. It seemed the fluffs at the horizon were whisking by at higher speed, although it was relatively calm outside his house. A trick of light, he thought.

Warren turned way from the window, dressed, and went downstairs to discover more damage — an overturned chair, some broken knick-knacks, and his study was a mess — before deciding to venture out to check the neighbours — two other people — Raymond, whose house shared the brow of a small hill with him, and old Tom, who lived in a smaller cottage cozily nestled into the slight slope beneath them.

Behind and above their houses was a ruined folly, a tall stone finger that gestured toward the heavens. A narrow lane wound up the hill from the valley roadway and ended in a cul-de-sac for him and Raymond, whom he noticed was already outside, trying without success to shovel the fluff from his driveway. Every time he attempted to scoop up the fluffy stuff it floated away, and when he was able to collect some, it refused to be thrown to the side and simply drifted back to the ground in front of him.

"Good luck with that," Warren called out, and his neighbour turned and waved his shovel at him.

"Don't worry, I do have a better idea," Raymond called back, and returned to his open garage. He reappeared with a large electric fan in his hands. He faced it along the driveway, gave Warren the thumbs up signal, and turned it on. It was difficult to see the results as the blast of air thrashed the fluff into a maelstrom of turbulent whiteness which rose and curled back and then simply seemed to hang in the air, blocking the view before ever so quietly subsiding and mixing into the regular fall of downy white. Experimenting with his aim, he achieved some success and after a few minutes of blowing the surface of the driveway was visible again, and Raymond gave him another thumbs up and began to walk with the fan, cleaning the white off their shared hedge, which blew up a thick cloud of fuzz that swirled in and around Warren's porch. He tried to call to Raymond to stop and inadvertently caught a few flakes in his mouth, only to discover the cottony material had a distinctly unpleasant, metallic taste. It reminded him of a copper penny. He spit out his saliva and retreated inside the house where he ate some food to quell the aftertaste and then retreated into his study to replace the fallen books to their shelves. When he went to bed the white flakes were still falling heavily.

Warren awoke the next day to discover the wall of whiteness was now almost to the top of his bay windows, although it was hard to tell as the speed of the drifting particles had increased and it appeared the top foot of flakes were now being blown by the strong wind he saw earlier. He had just finished lunch when he heard a knock and opened the door to reveal neighbour Raymond wearing a wide face mask, swimming goggles, and completely covered in white.

"Ray, you look like a drowned ghost," he said, somewhat surprised, "or maybe a short Yeti. Come in." He waved Raymond into the house. The flakes dissolved without melting.

He led his neighbour into the kitchen, made a pot of tea, and waited for Raymond to reveal the reason for his visit.

"I thought I'd check on you, being the new neighbour in the, ah, neighbourhood." Raymond took a few sips, and Warren nodded affirmatively.

"I'm fine, Raymond, no complaints. I have shelves of food and a library of books. Sustenance for body and mind. You look fine — clever outfit — say, have you checked in with old Tom?"

He wondered why Raymond was suddenly concerned about his well-being. They weren't really friends, and Warren certainly wasn't new to the area, although he couldn't exactly remember when he arrived. He didn't have much in common with his two neighbours, being the quiet literary type as opposed to the loud and gossipy Raymond or old Tom, who stalked the grounds like a Norwegian Forest cat and incessantly fingered his necklace of runes. Regardless, he saw both of them virtually every day as they worked in the three gardens. Like clockwork they would appear each morning to cut, trim, weed, water, and plant until taking a break at noon. Two hours later they were at it again, this time including his yard in their horticultural assaults. He wasn't interested in cultivation, so he never bothered his volunteer gardeners, preferring to stay indoors and let them keep the area in chocolate box condition.

Raymond nodded. "Don't worry about old Tom. I talked to him yesterday and he's fine. Which is to say he's still as crazy as ever."

"Crazy?" Warren laughed slightly. He thought both of them were odd. "How so?"

"You know he's always been a yappy old codger. Likes to boss me around — don't put those lilies there! — and he likes to pretend he's the king of the hill, even though my house is the highest."

Warren took a sip to hide his smile.

"I'd just call that, ohh, eccentric."

"Big ego, more likely," Raymond said. "He likes his dramas."

"Why was he different yesterday?"

Raymond leaned in, closer to Warren.

"He seemed even more nutty than usual. Kept repeating over and over it was all his fault and he should have been more careful."

"I don't understand."

"Neither do I, and I don't think I've ever heard him admit to a mistake. A bit of a perfectionist, he is. Likes to keep things tidy and neat. Especially these yards. You know what — I figure he made a trimming mistake on one of his precious cherry trees. You know he's a master pruner. He'll tell you even if you don't ask."

Warren had noticed their division of duties. Tom and Raymond split their yard work into two distinct categories

— Raymond did all the planting and Tom did the trimming and mowing. It was a good system, and Warren had noticed the two gardeners rarely worked together but covered separate territories as a sort of horticultural ying-yang, with Raymond the artistic force and Tom following, keeping all under control.

"Perhaps an overly sensitive master pruner. Still seems like much ado …"

"His whining could be about anything, Warren — that's a guess." Raymond got up and wandered over to the window. The flakes continued to blow around. He turned and pointed his teacup at Warren.

"Don't be fooled. Tom looks old and wise but don't let him start on you with his magic runes. He believes all that Norwegian nonsense. Like his odd-ball yarn about something called — let me get this right — a *fimbulwinter*. A sort of very bad storm. He says he started it. Pure manure, as far as I'm concerned."

"Sounds ominous," Warren said, "maybe that's why he's upset."

Raymond nodded slowly. "Yes, that's certainly possible. See, I told you he was crazy."

Warren stroked his chin. "Can't say Tom ever said anything to me about an impending storm, but I think this whiteout might be around for awhile. It's still coming down."

He looked out the window. "You and Tom will have some time off from gardening for awhile."

Raymond said nothing, but Warren caught a flicker of anxiety cross his face. Declining another cup of tea, he thanked Warren for his hospitality, put on his goggles and mask, and disappeared into a wall of fluffy white that had quietly grown to at least eight feet tall. Warren wondered if he would see him again.

A few days later Warren made the happy realization the snow was slowing. After a strong horizontal flow, the wind's speed had dropped, and gravity was again flaunting its undying attraction among the flakes. Warren had been happy to ignore the storm as it silently raged, but now with the situation improving he felt a growing compulsion to get out and explore a bit, maybe even visit Raymond.

He organized his kit — goggles, mask, compass, coil of string — and looked out past his porch. The snow was still at least a foot over his head, and he had three steps to descend to the ground. He ate a brief lunch, cleaned the dishes, and prepared to go. Compass. Check. North was always pointing to the folly on the hill. Mask, goggles on. Just before he stepped into the fluffy oblivion, he tied one end of the string to the front door handle.

He walked into the whiteness.

The feeling was half exhilaration, half disbelief. Warren was expecting some weight, some resistance. There was none. It was just like walking through air, albeit an impossibly thick, brilliantly white miasma of tiny bits of swirling nothingness. His vision stopped at the glass of his goggles, and he was in a silence so profound he could soon hear internal sounds … breathing, heartbeat, tinnitus. Given the zero visibility he found it easier to walk with his eyes closed, one hand stretched out before him like a stumbling zombie, the other spooling out the string.

He followed his mental map to Raymond's house and within a few minutes successfully bumped into the garage. Crushing Raymond's prized flowers underfoot, Warren made it around the building and pulled up the garage door. The car was gone. The big fan sat by the doorway to the kitchen. He knocked loudly but there was no answer. The door was unlocked. He left his gear there and entered the house. Inside, he found the place surprisingly empty, save for a drawing room that looked unused, and a snug with a chair, table, typewriter and, if Warren could believe his eyes, an old record player. He had heard of them, but never seen one. He turned it on. The disc dropped, the tone arm swung and lowered itself. A chorus of voices began: "If you go down to the woods today…" Startled, he turned it off, and the song slowly died with a long "you're inn forrrah biiig surrr…".

He picked up Raymond's fan before following his string home, and after storing it in his garage he thought about eating but didn't feel that hungry. He wondered where Raymond might have gone, and why he didn't also leave a note in Raymond's house should he return. No matter, it would be easy to make a second trip when and if necessary.

He still felt like exploring the neighbourhood but realized wandering around within this white blindness would be stupid, if not suicidal. He pondered the possibilities of walking on the snow. A sort of special oversized snowshoe to distribute his weight. No, he realized, he couldn't get anything that big out of any upstairs window. Perhaps if the drifts decreased. That meant more waiting. He briefly considered attaching Raymond's fan to the front of his car and possibly running it off the car battery to blow away enough snow so he could see the road, but he didn't really know how to do that with his limited resources. He nevertheless made a final attempt to use the car's battery to power the fan — attaching both to a small wagon — but succeeded only in breaking off one of the battery's terminals. Out of ideas, he retired to his study to read.

Over the next few days the falling fluff slowed to a few random flakes, and the drifts outside seemed to contract somewhat, although Warren had no idea where the fuzz might have gone. Did it evaporate? Outside, the wall of white was still over his head. His urge to get out and explore was still strong, and he finally decided simply walking was his best choice and he strung together all the string he could find on a stick of wood. He suited up, connected the twine to the door handle, and headed due north to the lane. He found it easily and turned right, heading down the hill.

He discovered he could feel his way along by testing the right curb with a foot. At the first curve he bumped into the back of Raymond's car, a white loaf of bread blocking the road, and a quick search revealed Raymond wasn't in it. He kept following the road's curve and came across the driveway to Tom's cottage. He turned right again and finally reached the house.

After knocking and waiting for about a minute Warren tried the handle. It opened. He entered a hall with a living room to the left, and like Raymond's house it also seemed unused. Opposite was the kitchen diner. It looked untouched. He wandered down the hall and investigated the next room, a bedroom with a body on the bed.

It was Tom, his old neighbour, lying on his back with his eyes still open. Warren stood by the bed and offered a few words of condolence before closing the man's eyes. He noticed a slight green hue in Tom's flesh and checked his fingertips to see if anything had rubbed off. The rest of the house was empty — he wondered why both Tom and Raymond had little or no furniture — but still took the time to explore the kitchen and pantry for any useful food. He picked out a few favourites and put them in his bag. The garage did have a car in it — there were no supplies in the trunk — and after closing the door behind him Warren re-entered the fluff and rewound his string back home.

Over the next week Warren watched the whiteness dissipate, drank tea, and read every morning in his study. The blanket of white had dissipated to about three feet deep, and he had often taken afternoon walks around the neighbourhood, wondering if he might meet anyone, and watching to see if any road traffic had returned.

On a whim, he decided one day to explore the folly itself. It was round, fashioned of limestone, and according to local legend was created by a now forgotten landowner as a signal to the king. The stone tube rose at least 30 feet above the hilltop, and after careful climbing Warren found himself at the cramped summit. All around him the albino landscape gently fell away in a series of classic farmland hillocks and depressions, and he could just see the local town nestled in a far-off valley, its giant red shopping mall dome poking up like an angry boil in the hazy distance.

Carefully retracing his steps, he left the folly and explored the grounds, ultimately saddened to find two bodies sprawled on the little commons that encircled the hill. Warren couldn't tell how long they had been dead, but they looked more like abandoned mannequins than people, lying on their backs with eyes open and neutral expressions. Even more strangely, like old Tom neither of them looked like they had been dead very long, with clean features and no signs of decomposition. He also noticed a slight green tinge to their faces, a sort of weather-beaten copper patina. He dragged them into whatever shelter the folly might provide and made a mental note to contact the police when the snow had gone.

Warren didn't have to wait long. Within a week the fluff had disappeared, and the usual vista of green trees, greener grass, hedges, and flowers became his daily outlook. Once again, he awoke to the familiar sounds of far-off traffic, the chitter of hedge clippers and drone of a lawn mower. Without fanfare Raymond had simply reappeared one morning, gave Warren a thumbs up, and proudly unveiled a new wheelbarrow full of potting soil and various seedlings.

There was a new neighbour in the lower cottage, too, and she surprised Warren with a visit to introduce herself as Skadi, old Tom's niece from a village in rural Norway. She was a pleasant lady, a middle-aged spinster with a quiet, yet coy demeanour that suggested a more libertine past. Warren was intrigued. Raymond was happy.

Like her uncle, old Tom, Skadi proved to be an obsessive and tireless gardener, and within a few days she had joined Raymond in their daily yard work. Her specialty was topiary, and she was soon sizing up the boxwood and laurel bushes in all three yards. Happy things were back to normal, Warren walked down to the highway, caught a bus to town and organized the purchase and delivery of a new car battery. He also remembered to report the strange bodies he had found at the folly to the proper authorities.

Over the next few months Warren resumed his old habit of rising mid-morning, eating a light breakfast, and then retreating to his study to read. After lunch he would wander the neighbourhood, often stopping at the ruined folly before heading home for afternoon tea.

Skadi would often arrive for a visit and a cuppa around this time, still warm from yard work and often with bits of juniper clinging to her long blonde hair. Her skill with garden shears Warren found amazing, and she had already transformed the high hedge along his property line into a line of finely carved running reindeer.

He wondered if Santa on a sleigh would be next.

One afternoon she showed up with a wooden box.

"Please come in, tea is made." Warren led her into the drawing room.

"Here, this is for you." Skadi held out the box for Warren. "Careful, it's heavier than it looks."

It was weighty and Warren carefully put it on the coffee table. He stopped to admire the box itself, beautifully carved with motifs of holly leaves and mistletoe. He lifted the fitted top and was somewhat surprised to see the top of a glass dome.

"What's this?" he asked. "A child's toy?"

Skadi sat in an armchair, poured herself a cup of tea, took a sip, and motioned to Warren to sit down.

"A couple days ago I finally got around to going through my uncle's garage and I found this box with a note in it. Basically, it said this is the container for the globe, and that if anything happened to Tom, both globe and box were to go to you."

"Really? But I'm sort of flattered — I can't remember receiving an inheritance before."

"Keep it safe," she advised Warren, "it's not really an inheritance. Uncle Tom indicated it was your turn to protect it."

After she left, and unsure of her warning, Warren carefully placed the box on a shelf in his study. Over dinner he thought that Old Tom must have gone a little crazy with the whiteout — Raymond may have been correct — and had regressed to obsessing on some infantile object of assurance, like a child's toy, which Tom felt should be preserved for some reason. Perhaps it was also from Norway. He wondered if Tom might have used the word 'protect' with a different meaning, like 'don't break.' It all seemed rather silly, and he had forgotten about it by the morning.

The next few months passed peacefully. Raymond tended the flowers and Skadi sculpted the neighbourhood into a Norwegian fantasy of evergreen delights. Every morning Warren puttered around his house before retreating to his library to read. He had an extensive library, meticulously organized into categories and genres. Having just successfully solved a closed-door mystery, he leaned back in his chair, his mind wandering over a range of interests as he vaguely scanned his books, finally pausing at a finely carved box at the dark end of a shelf. What was that? He recognized old Tom's gift. Didn't it come with a warning of some sort? What had Skadi said ... protect it? From what, Warren wondered. The wooden case was thick and padded. Thieves? Highly unlikely here in the deep rural hinterlands. Perhaps there was something special about it — or was it just another of old Tom's runic fantasies. Warren didn't usually feel intrigue, but this little mystery was enough to cause him to rise and bring the box back to his desk. He removed the lid and carefully raised the globe from its container. It was big, mostly empty, not round but slightly lozenge-shaped, and sat deeply in its carved wooden base, which was also decorated with spiky holly leaves and mistletoe berries. The globe and box were made by the same hand, Warren realized. How old was it? He guessed it might well be worth a tidy sum in the antique toy market.

He put the globe down on a table and looked inside it. Whatever was there was hard to see in the study, so he took it to the drawing room's big bay window. The sun was shining in, brightly yellow. Holding the globe waist high and looking straight down into it, he could make out a green, rural scene, as if viewed from a considerable height. A hill was off to one side, with some kind of structures around it, and on the other, a town nestled in a valley. He wondered if this was old Tom's home in Norway. A souvenir from his youth, perhaps?

Warren looked again, closely from the side. He could make out squiggles that appeared to be roads, and a meandering blue line he supposed was a river. Not much else. He thought if this was a toy, it certainly appeared to be quite boring. No big trees, no picturesque house, no animals, nothing really for any child's eye to cling to. He paused. It was an antique kid's snow globe, but he could see no snow. Warren expected to see some white flakes lying on the ground, ready to be agitated, but all was green. After some head turning and squinting, he finally noticed a thick, dark slit running along the edge of the globe between the glass and the miniature landscape. Was the snow hiding there, under the nondescript scene at the base of the glass? Very clever. How much was hidden away? The base was quite large. On an impulse, he held the globe up to the sunlight and revolved it three times counterclockwise. One turn each for himself, Skandi and Raymond. It worked. A tsunami of white crested up the inside of the globe and Warren laughed as the flakes reached the top, mixed, and spread out, forming fantastic patterns under the glass.

A moment later the room swayed round, and Warren

twisted to the floor, barely clutching the globe to his chest. Something smashed on the floor behind him. He curled into a fetal position, protecting the globe and himself from falling debris. When the spinning stopped, Warren carefully regained his footing and looked out the window.

It was all white out.

POSSESSION

Subject: Well, Well, Well
From: Virginia
To: Frank

Well, Well, Well.

Mike and I were emailing and he mentioned you had a web site. Well I took a look, and what should my wondering eyes behold, but, MY PHOTOGRAPHS!!!! Yeeeeesssss Sirree Frankiee!!! Well now I admit I always believed you had kept those photos and negatives even though you denied it, but TIME'S UP!!!

Those are my personal property and I want them back. Interesting for me to find that this still pisses me off after all this time, but art is art, and that is my art you're exhibiting without so much as a by your leave never mind a byline.

After you return my negatives to me, you may continue to use the photos on your website but I expect to see my business name, Natural Designs, beneath them. The least you can do.

I look forward to receiving my negatives soon. My business address is attached.

Subject: Re: Well, Well, Well
From: Frank
To: Virginia

I return from a trip to find yr rant of last Sunday pm ...

Quite the surprise! What's it been ... since 1985? Sometimes you wonder if any old paths will cross, but this is outta the blue. 20 freakin' years.

So, you've seen my music website. With your photos?

Sorry, Virginia, but you can bitch & self-righteously whine all you want, but had you looked closely at the images I've posted, you would have noted they are merely scans of the pix which ran with my reviews in *The Big Smoke Express* ... there are no negatives, there are no prints. I have no idea where any of that stuff could be ... As for credits, well, sure ... I gave 'em to Mike ... I can give 'em to you ... Now I know you're still alive ...

I've checked my *Big Smoke Express* files, and the only pix of yours that actually deserve credit are the Bowie shots from 1983. Quite the night. But don't forget that these pix, as well as the interviews, ultimately belong to the newspaper. You got paid. You want a copyright hassle with them? Good luck with the new owners.

If I did have any remaining stuff of yours it probably got destroyed in 1997 ... I was living in a condo downtown, and I had so much stuff I decided to put it in storage ... an old brick joint out on Dupont. I still remember coming back from a vacation and noticing an item in the paper: storage building burns for a week. It was my storage building. I lost a lot of memorabilia in that blaze ... a real mind-wrencher.

As for crediting these shots as being done by your business, that seems a tad overzealous. My pages are for my profit, so I may have to struggle with your desire to promote yourself today with work done 20 years ago ... and as for you giving me "permission," well, it's always great to start the day off with a laugh ...

What exactly do you design, anyway?

As for me, yes, surprisingly I've done well. It's great to retire young. But then, being a self-indulgent jerk having nostalgic fun after a successful career should broaden your smile, no? Who woulda guessed?

I also see you live fairly close ... Scarborough. Lose a contest? You know, I never wondered where you finally ended up ... so maybe I'll drive over for a visit. I promise not to gloat ...

And, of course, credits are as credits do. Check it out ....

Subject: [Fwd: Well, Well, Well]
From: Frank
To: Dr DNA

Doctor ... get yr harp out ... it's time to sing the blues ...

Blast from the ancient past, man ... check out this crazy email I just got from the apparently still alive Virginia ...

Done? Can you believe it, man? Talk about a friggin t-bolt from deep space ... like an ethereal email ghost ... and she lives close!

I've included the email I sent her back ... self-explanatory ... OK, sure ... maybe a little heavy on the "I'm OK — you're not" digs, but yeah, she did take some of the pix ... but I don't have 'em ...the posted shots were scanned from my copies of the old *BX* ...

Jeez ... man ... I still can't quite believe it ... whatta zap ... I musta stared at her name on my email for a minute before I opened it ... surreal ... I don't think you ever really knew her ... how many times did you see her? Five? We were opposites, remember? Should never, ever have married her ... always felt roped into that ... shit, what was I thinking?

And then I find out she's got round heels.

101

Subject: do you know?
From: Frank
To: Mike

Miguel, hear you're back from Mexico City ... *Bienvenido de vuelta* to Toronto! Maybe some shit hitting the fan here ... check out the email I got from, of all people, Virginia.

Question for you ... did she simply email you out of the blue looking for me ... or are you getting oral sex from her in exchange for info? She's now freaking out on me over no credits on my site for her crummy rock pix ... like I didn't ask for "permission," — that was good for a laugh ... interesting, tho ... first contact in over 20 years! Maybe I should say first opportunity for me to gloat in 20 years ... ha

What it is that Natural Designs actually designs?

Subject: Re: do you know?
From: Mike
To: Frank

Oh, I mentioned to her that you had a website and told her to check it out, I didn't expect this kind of reaction!

Better hire Clarence Darrow.

Yes, I have returned from CDMX ... not at all what I expected ... but at least my Spanish has improved.

Subject: Design?
From: Frank
To: Mike

Again, what it is that Natural Designs actually designs?

Subject: Re: Design?
From: Mike
To: Frank

Hard to describe, it involves doing store windows and also being involved with craft fairs and trade shows. Sounds like a good racket from what I've heard.

Subject: Re: Design?
From: Frank
To: Mike

Interesting ... last I heard Virginia was a waitress at some Greek restaurant on the Danforth ... the craft thing goes way back ... she was making candles in the 70s. Well, I've heard nada back ...

Subject: "My photos..."
From: Dr DNA
To: Frank

What photos? What does she mean? The occasional rock 'n' roll thing? Did she really take them? Or is it the usual argument in such cases?

And Frankie — since when is "photography" art? Anyone can point and click ... but to draw the same thing, well it's like saying: my car is nice, it's art; I drive, therefore I'm an artist. By the way, did you steal her negatives? Naughty, naughty.

Subject: games
From: Frank
To: Dr DNA

No response yet from Virginia ... can you believe that shit? More than 20 years later and not much has changed ... but now I know where she lives ... metaphorically ... so let the games begin ... remember, I told you I had a feeling I was being tracked ... nothing like getting wired over a handful of over-exposed b&ws. Ha ha I'm still laughing.

Subject: web impact
From: Dr DNA
To: Frank

Did I tell you about Mike? He's emailed me, says he was threatened re his Mexico City piece — some gangster read it, threatens death. So he's abandoned it, he says.

I said, you want me to take it down from my travel site 'til you get back? No, he says. Leave it. That sorta screws up the journal I was planning, too.

Don't know if he's exaggerating or not. Might be his attitude — says he can't get into the whole macho mode.

Don't e-mail him about this.

Subject: Re: My Photographs
From: Frank
To: Virginia
You stunned into silence?

Subject: Re: My Photographs
From: Virginia
To: Frank
Having taken the time to investigate, I have confirmed that *The Big Smoke Express*, paying me $125 for rights to publish the photos, not paying me a wage, and not retaining the negatives, were indeed entitled to what is referred to as first time publishing rights only.

According to the Copyright Law I retain the rights to all publication until 50 years after the developing of the negatives. Unfortunately, I do not have the negatives of the Bowie photos. Please remove my pictures from your website as I am not comfortable with your use of them.

Subject: Re: My Photographs
From: Frank
To: Virginia
As the Firesign Theatre used to say:

Nick Danger: "What kind of chump do you take me for?"

Nancy: "First class."

Subject: Re: My Photographs
From: Virginia
To: Frank

Indeed you're probably are a chump, however that was not my point. I have always missed the negatives from these concerts. Apparently my shoe box full of negs has mysteriously gone "up in smoke." Remember the box? When I opened it up after leaving you it was full of different photos. I thought then you might have made the old switcheroo, but shit, I grabbed that photo stuff first on my way out the door. Didn't figure you were smart enough to think ahead.

As it happens the many shots of David you used were stored in the box, which twigged my curiosity. And suspicions. If you have those negatives, and I find out for sure, there will be holy hell to pay. I'll take your fuckin ass to court, or sic some of my more burly friends on your tail. I repeat, please remove my pictures from your web site. NOW. Thank you. Not.

Subject: holy shit
From: Frank
To: Mike

That zany Virginia is still at it. Accusations will soon fly ... and all the offending pix have to be removed ... pissoff as they are the big clickbait.

Do you actually converse with her on a regular basis? How did this all come up? I get a sort of ill-defined "stalker" vibe off this.

Subject: Re: holy shit
From: Mike
To: Frank

Beats me, I haven't heard anything from her since I (sorry) spilled the beans about all this a few weeks ago, despite sending a couple of e-mails.

Subject: She can take a leap
From: Frank
To: Dr DNA

I've attached her latest rants from yesterday and this am … christ, it's like some harpy from the mist, emerging after 20 years to shriek and wail and demand retribution … what the fuck is she gonna do? Sue me? Statute of Limitations, baby. Besides, those pix are all scans from the *BX* … I'm gonna suggest she go back under her rock and disappear for another 20 years.

Subject: Virginia Negatives
From: Dr DNA
To: Frank

Jesus — she isn't very happy about this, is she?

Subject: what next?
From: Frank
To: Dr DNA

Is she pissed off? Sure, and it's great … but I'm watching her carefully … I've been pondering the past … this whole thing has got me thinking … she was always a few steps ahead … I always found out about stuff after the fact.

OK, maestro … what would you do?

Subject: she's askin for it
From: Dr DNA
To: Frank

She's begging to be whipped. Question: David Bowie, does he care about the expropriation of his image?

Fact: you're fine.

Fact: she takes you to court — civil limitation here is two years. No go.

Fact: she's threatened you. Save that email.

Suppose the male chauvinist pig would say her assault

is a "desperate cry for help." Well, after that last e-mail, the direct command to cease & desist — maybe I'd be silent for a week or two, then say, what do you want? Well, games. Bullshit. You don't need it. History is on yr side — Virginia made a bad choice. Now she's trying to prove it wasn't. Cut her the slack she doesn't deserve.

Subject: OK, I'll relent
From: Frank
To: Dr DNA
    Doktor: Silent for a week or two? … but why wait? Sounds like she only wants all the pix removed and is suspicious about the negs … especially the Bowie pix she took at the party after the gig … she's always liked that best … so I take it down … is that going to stop people from reading the review? What am I saying? People want images, not opinions. Now I'm contrite and emasculated.

Subject: Virginia Roll
From: Dr DNA
To: Frank
    Yes, rolling over. Rich guy like you, I'd go further — offer her a thousand bucks, say, look babe, we were a unit then, who knows who owns/did what? But I'll put a link/give you a joint credit. Don't want to fight with you, babe. Then was then.
    Thus she becomes an ex-mistress.
    "The Man Who Understands Women."

Subject: How Much?
From: Frank
To: Dr DNA
    $1,000 ????????????
    Let's not cut off our balls to spite our dicks.

Subject: other people's $$
From: Dr DNA
To: Frank

Just love giving away other people's dough, is all — be grandiose, round everything out in zeros.

Plus I drank a bottle of Barollo last night — don't feel grandio this morning.

A page out of Nick Pallodan's book — whenever you screw up or cross the line, just open yr wallet. The sulky faces give way to righteousness, then greed. Works every time. Hey, his ex is still working like a slave in his office. And his ex-mistress is still running errands for him. Just lay low. Silence, exile and cunning.

Subject: Re: Virginia Roll
From: Frank
To: Dr DNA

OK ... I think I'll take some of your advice and run silent, run deep for a couple weeks ... either that or simply take the bloody pictures down and just forget about it ... altho I do feel a strange attraction to screwing her around a bit ... those pix are really from the *BX* ... does she have proof of ownership over something so nebulous as pix in an underground paper from 20 years ago?

I just hate to give in so, well, quickly.

Subject: OK
From: Frank
To: Virginia

Enuff blather about negs, photos, copyrights, personal property, comfort zones ... blah, blah, blah

Check out the offending web pages. I've given you appropriate credit, plus an email link.

The Bowie pages get about 5750 hits a day (mostly 16-year-olds in Tokyo), so you might actually get an email or two ... maybe you can sell them some "design." Now, will you please sink back into the mists of time and quit disturbing me?

PS: just as an aside, here's my take on the legality of all this. While we were married, all property was joint property, including all negs, photos, interviews, etc. After the Decree Absolute, a line was drawn in the sand. What you owned at that moment was what you owned. No more claims. If I have the negs, they're mine. If you have the negs, they're yours. Considering how well you cleaned me out in 1986, I'm very surprised you might have missed anything ... but no matter.

Bottom line, I own the *Big Smoke Express* papers from which these images and interviews were scanned. I have no photographs or negatives to give you. As I said before, I'll be happy to give you credit for the action of taking the pix, just as I gave Mike credit for co-authoring some of the interviews, but it ends after that.

Now, go away.

Subject: Re: OK
From: Virginia
To: Frank

I want all the negatives, which I can prove are mine, especially the David Bowie. Get it off your sight. You were repelent then and you are repelent now. As my old friend Stan (you might remember him) said over a coffee the other day, "Why have anything to do with this asshole?"

Subject: spellcheck?
From: Frank
To: Virginia

Hey ...

That's "site", not "sight"... and it's "repellent," not "repelent"...

I agree with Stan — why do you care? Stan ... wasn't

he that university prof, the one you used to screw on your "weekend trips with the girls?"

David doesn't remember you, and you know that ...

PS: over the last couple days, as I've pondered your unilateral demands and general bad humour — which I've responded to — I've been interrupted by a single thought, which keeps creeping around the periphery: what's really happening? Why the call to Mike? Why mention me? Why the concern over an ancient photo? It's been a long time.

After 20 years ... well, who are you? Our brief liaison seems like another age, another life ... your infidelity is a forgotten memory of the past ... as it happened, my working career followed you, and my student career proceeded you, so you're really only present in a thin slice of my memories — those underground newspaper days of laughs, drugs and rock 'n' roll ... fun, but fleeting ... and then reality rolled in and I became a successful stockbroker.

Virginia ... you're a now-faded being from the past ... made even more ethereal by the disembodied email ... I see no face, hear no voice, have no knowledge about your life ... and, oddly enuff, I have no interest in reacquainting myself with it or you.

Let it go ... then was then ... now is now...

Who am I? Certainly not the young rock 'n' roll writer you once fucked over and left ... really, this has brought back memories ... in 1985 the deal was I was the boring jerk interested in a music industry career, and you were the antsy, artsy party girl who liked rock stars ... these silly old out-of-focus, grainy b&w prints of yours aren't really that important, are they? What's this really all about? A single picture? No ... what's important? Not still David bloody Bowie.

Subject: One Lasst Time!!
From: Virginia
To: Frank

If you refuse to remove MY PHOTOGRAPHS from your sight, I will have to take further measures. Your being a real prick about this. You've lied to me about the David Bowie negs to get back at me. I know it.

Subject: Amateur writers
From: Frank
To: Dr DNA

Why is Virginia so upset? I figgered it out: her chemistry factory is breaking down, man ... it's menopause! Check her latest splutter ... the amateur always shows too much because the emotional imperative always overwhelms technique. Mike is also involved, and he's desperately trying to keep the lowest of profiles ... like Sgt Schultz, she sees nothing, knows nothing.

Subject: Freudian slippage
From: Dr DNA
To: Frank

She spells "site" as "sight." The problem with e-mail is not its disposition towards grammatical error, but rather its unconscious confession of the truth.

It was those extra insults included in the "let's make a deal and now fuck off" message that did it.

As the song says, "A hiss is just a hiss ..." (*As Time Goes By*)

Subject: My Site Got Checked
From: Frank
To: Dr DNA

Jesus, man ... I was checking my web stats last nite and I notice this odd url ... so I boot it up and shit, it's an internet copyright investigation centre. Hire out to musicians, mostly ... record companies ... some authors, movies ... if you copy it, they're lookin' for you. And, of course, you've got keywords popping out of the seams on your portal page ... well ... they've visited ... wait & see time.

Subject: copyright cops
From: Dr DNA
To: Frank
What did I say? Only a question of time. You're not using the Steely Dan tune anymore are you? Might get after you over any number of lifts. But they might be on the track of those rock star photos, even tho' music is their professed beat.

I'm sure my site has been checked for the digi movie clips. However, as they are used exclusively in support of the film features, there should be no complaints.

The good ole days of "open source" on the Net are over.

Subject: Post-Napster policing reopens ISP wounds
From: Dr DNA
To: Frank
This CNET Investor story has been sent to you from Doctor@suture.ca

This might add some light to the MIBs who checked you out.

Facing the prospect of a post-Napster world, tension is starting to build between copyright holders and Internet service providers over who should police other file-swapping networks that are poised to step in as replacements.

Subject: Private Eyes
From: Frank
To: Dr DNA
This ain't no napster thing, man ... this is typical Virginia

Horror Show. Notice how she works: the frantic opening, the slow twist as your options diminish, then the final threatening stance. You could make a movie of it. Next thing, she'll be renting an apartment across the street and checking my schedule before she pulls a freakin B&E ... she wants those negs, man ... she wants 'em bad ... perfect!

Subject: Rage/Groupie e-book
From: Dr DNA
To: Frank

Was thinking, this photo thing has the potential for something like Cameron Crowe's *Almost Famous* (which I haven't seen), a nice nostalgic reprise of 60's rock scene.

Starts with the e-mail — and the demand — and this leads to "recollections" of the relationship. You could go hardcore, make her a groupie — who the journalist encounters in the scene (at a concert, say) — as the e-mail exchanges develop, so does the "recollection."

Her Toronto location — the city is great, but maybe not fictional enough — might be in the Mississippi Delta — how did she end up there? Etc.

Things escalate — she puts the Internet Police onto the guy. Why the hatred, why the obsession? Why in particular the pic of a certain star — this could be the "key" to it all.

Of course you might not want to go too deeply into this as the memories might be too much of a pissoff. Who needs agro in retirement?

Woke up thinking about it — the story has great potential.

Subject: bow wow bowie
From: Frank
To: Dr DNA

I've already thot about it…I'm already agro'ed …

I dunno if I ever told you, but what finally put Virginia

and I over the edge was the '83 Bowie concert ... she was wildly into the *Serious Moonlight* man he was peddling at the time ... she loved that upper-class brit crap ... the evening goes smooth ... we pick up our backstage passes, she takes all these shots at the concert, then we went back to Bowie's hotel for the usual fest of booze, dope, and horny flacks with their hands full of groupies.

Gotta tell ya — usually these after-gig parties were fun ... everybody was still wired from the performance ... everybody pissed ... the real drunks are droppin stuff off the balcony into the swimming pool 20 stories below ... shades of *Gimmie Shelter* ... Virginia heads off to check the scene, but I get led into the kitchen by the tour rep, a smooth brit with big pinkie rings and friggin pink shoes, who tells me he has set up an interview with the Bowie knife himself ... he'll find me when the Duke is ready ... so I do the rounds, have a few pops, blow a little weed and check out the scene.

I'm now noticing Virginia is nowhere to be found ... I check with the flack, and he says she and DB are in an adjoining room ... apparently she's taking pictures of him, and he doesn't want to be disturbed. There's nobody guarding the door, so I crack open the door to discover both lying on the bed, naked.

I couldn't believe it.

Virginia's looking surprised as hell ... the very thin duke gives a vague smile ... some heavies appear, grab me and shut the door. I didn't go nuts on her afterwards, but that was pretty well it for our bizarre friggin relationship.

Subject: Doctor One Down
From: Dr DNA
To: Mike

You know about Frank's hassles with Virginia in the old days? Here's the email about her and Bowie he just sent me.

Subject: Re: Doctor One Down
From: Mike
To: Dr DNA

Yeah. I know about all this crap. After she left him, I was out with Frankie one nite for drinks, and just as we were getting comfy at the bar and checking out the menu, up comes one of Virginia's old girlfriends. She said she had heard about her split, and said it was best for Frank as Virginia apparently had started screwing around very soon after their marriage. Not just musicians. Their friends. Like Stan, her old prof.

Frank couldn't believe it. He knew about the Bowie incident, but that was all. He was almost physically ill. Couldn't even drink. You know him: possessive as hell.

When he found out he had been wandering around with horns, he simply lost it. Stupid fuck. Complained of a sharp tightening in his guts. He couldn't eat. I watched that go on for three months. He shredded 45 pounds. Finally had to go to the doctor for some appetite pills.

That was the friggin worst, man. That's what turned him from uncaring to unforgiving.

Subject: Let it go
From: Dr DNA
To: Frank

Hey, man, too bad about the Bowie incident. But it was a long time ago. You're happy now. You got the negs? Give 'em to her — bury the past. Dig a hole.

Subject: I'm cool...
From: Frank
To: Dr DNA

Oh, it's goin underground, all right ... I've waited a long, long time. But it looks like it's been worth it. This meal may be cold, but it's delicious.

No shit, those Bowie negatives are the "key" all right … they're Virginia's direct link to her old whacked-out world of groupie dreams. Who knows how many liaisons she had? By now, that sexcapade with Bowie has no doubt become the last supper of her ongoing obsession … you'd think everything fades with time … but with those photographs her worship of the god-man, her fictionalizing of the event, can be sharply frozen in time with the accuracy of a nikon lens.

Can't you just imagine? There she is … the obsessive completist with the major piece of her personal puzzle tantalizingly close … but still so far away … she's thinking it would be best if those negs were tossed away, because then they'd be gone, and they wouldn't itch so much. But maybe, she thinks, maybe they still do exist … and if they do, where have I put them and how can she possess them again?

Hope can be a cruel thing.

Because, of course, she has no hope.

Why? Because I have them.

Yes! I have all her old negatives. I switched that shoe box 20 years ago, right under her nose, and they're mine. And they're going to stay mine. Maybe one day I'll tell her … maybe soon … I'll tell her what she craves more than anything is here with me.

Then she'll know. Then she'll finally realize. Those images will always be … in my possession.

Subject: didja hear?
From: Dr DNA
To: Mike

Hey, mon. I'm sure you know but the white suit guys from the funny farm swooped in and grabbed Frank a couple days ago. Might be in the kookoo's nest for awhile. Some kind of delusional paranoia. Keeps asking for a shoe box. Seems like those photos had a very negative effect.

THE *ICARUS* INCIDENT

When the shock waves of Japanese dive bombers fell like UFOs on the sleepy American base of Pearl Harbour on December 7, 1941, the repercussions echoed all over the western coastline of North America, resulting in frantic moves to set up defenses against a probable Japanese air attack and possible landing attempt. The Royal Canadian Air Force base at Comox and the Navy's Pacific headquarters in Victoria stepped up coastal surveillance, and the Royal Engineers were soon busy constructing beach and gun embankments at strategic points along the long, undefended west coast of Vancouver Island.

The army constructed one such base atop a high hill which rose up from the shores of Long Beach, a long, deserted stretch of sand just north of the Alberni Inlet. The site was imposing and practical; from the top of the hill, 1,000 feet above the crashing surf, the radar detected evidence of any intrusion far out into the Pacific. The army cleared off the hilltop and erected three utilitarian concrete buildings: one for a gun, one for the seven men who would monitor the horizon, and one for the massive radar eye.

Locals at the fishing town of Ucuelet, 20 miles to the south, called the place Sea Lion Mountain — because of the close proximity of sea lion colonies on small rocky islands just offshore — but the army liked to have things fit in with its own code, so they simply called the facility Radio Station Three, shortened to RS3.

In the official records RS3 saw no action in the Pacific conflict, although one town south of the inlet, Bamfield, was shelled for 20 minutes by a Japanese submarine in an attempt to knock out the Trans-Pacific communications cable, which was being used at the time to ferry high-priority information from Hawaii to Canada. According to local newspaper reports, the sub suddenly surfaced one afternoon and calmly began pumping cannon shells into the general business and residential area. Japanese information concerning the cable must have been poor, because the town was located nearly a half-mile from the squat concrete station which sucked the cable up from the sea.

After inflicting minor damage the Japanese sub disappeared as quietly as they had materialized. News of the attack prompted a red alert along the coastline, however, and several additional air sorties were arranged, and the Royal Navy cutter *Icarus*, armed with depth charges, pointed its sleek shape north on a special mission from Victoria to RS3.

--

The commander of the Japanese submarine *Nakano* was unhappy. The men he had sent out late last night to attack this dangerous radar station were not only late returning, but had not radioed in since reporting they were about to close in on the enemy. To make matters more complicated, his sonar technician had just reported the ping of an approaching ship. He was submerged in a shallow channel beside a rocky island covered with sea lions, but was hesitant about making any moves on the surface until his commando crew had made contact. With the rising sun he regretfully ordered his sub into deeper waters. Perhaps he would do better hunting bigger fish. He turned south and set course for the navy yards in Victoria.

--

I only became aware of my family's involvement in the Pacific war last year, when my maternal grandmother died and my parents gave me the stuff in her basement. The place was old and musty, and the haul consisted of several old chairs, a useless chesterfield, a few old trunks, and some boxes of old books. She wasn't a hoarder. It dawned on me the "gift" was probably a way for my folks to get the basement cleaned out, but the books and the one old sea trunk caught my attention right off, so I lugged them home first and made plans to deal with the rest later.

The books proved to be a dichotomy of vintage science fiction — the kind of stuff collectors crave — which I thought was odd considering my grandmother's reading tastes tended towards historical romance and the odd mystery novel, and what appeared to be textbooks on electrical engineering.

The trunk was locked, but the canvas had rotted around the clasp, and a few good tugs easily pulled the metal from its seams. It contained a few uniforms, a sheaf of letters from the navy, and diaries for the years 1941 and 1942. I was surprised to note the letters were addressed to my presumed-dead Uncle Mike, who mysteriously dropped out of sight in 1942. He was never seen again.

I remembered Uncle Mike only by reputation, as my teetotalling mother used to plague my father — who never refused a nip now and then — with warnings that if he kept drinking he'd go crazy like his brother, and she wasn't going to have any of that. The letters were mostly navy stuff. Official crap.

The diaries were more interesting, and after a quick flip through a few entries it soon became apparent the man who wrote these thoughts was a different personality than the drunken slob dragged about by my mother.

It was obvious a brain unsaturated with booze had been at work on these pages. Uncle Mike, who was into electronics before the war broke out, had been assigned to the *Icarus* as communications officer, and spent at least one year chasing submarines in the coastal waters of British Columbia before he simply went missing.

My father didn't have much of a relationship with his younger brother — the old man joined the air force as a fighter pilot, which he thought was superior to the navy — but he did embrace one idea which seemed to fixate the both of them, and that was a belief in the existence of Unidentified Flying Objects and aliens.

The old man had two stock UFO tales he used to lay out at parties, the first being Uncle Mike's adventures at RS3, and his own wartime contact with some UFOs called Foo Fighters, which were literally balls of fire that often harassed British, Canadian, and American pilots.

The French actually named them, using their word *feu* for fire, and the old man's only contact with the unexplained came when he was flying a routine mission with the 415th Night Fighter Squadron, flying a Mosquito on a bomber protection patrol over Germany in July, 1943. The story goes that at three in the morning, while escorting a wing of Lancasters back home, my father was astonished to see a bright orange glow climbing rapidly towards him. Afraid of rockets, he kicked the Mozzy into a series of evasive movements, but the glow stayed close to his right wingtip, finally blinking off after several minutes. The next day he and his navigator complained of sore eyes.

Apparently other pilots in the 415 had similar experiences, but during the war one never knew what was a new weapon and what wasn't. My father usually told that story with all seriousness. Was it an alien craft? Secret German weapon?

My Uncle Mike's UFO story was slowly distorted into absurdity as the years went on, and was always told for a laugh, but I remember the first time I heard it was at a party my folks threw when were living on an air base back in Canada. I would have been around 13 years old then. The

Illustration: Paul H. Williams

...my father was astonished to see a bright orange glow
climbing rapidly towards him...

old man was slightly drunk, just enough to attain a degree of eloquence, but his audience was thoroughly pissed. After awhile every line was met with gales of laughter, and the story was finally cut slightly short by my mother, sober and embarrassed, who suggested the time might be better spent playing charades.

It almost seemed like too much of a coincidence when, a few days later, I picked up the second of Uncle Mike's diaries and began scanning the entries. Most were short and technical about a short wave radio he was working on, but my attention was caught when the word Bamfield jumped off the page. I had often visited the sleepy coastal village on long weekends when I was a university student. The entries read:

July 10, 1942: Aboard the cutter *Icarus* off the west coast of Vancouver Island. Weather overcast and sea choppy. Already I'm frustrated with working on a shifting deck. Happily, I am making progress on improving these finicky electronics, despite the irritating rocking of the ship.

July 11, 1942: More news. Apparently Bamfield, the town just north of our present position, was shelled by a sub a few days ago and sustained minor damage. The locals, fishermen mostly, got all high and mighty about the attack and apparently had to be restrained from charging out in a few small boats to catch this enemy fish. Fat chance for success, but then again they might have been just bullshitting later in the pub long after the sub had left. The brass at headquarters were quite shocked. More work for us, it appears.

July 13, 1942: Yesterday we found a Japanese life jacket floating in the surf off the small coastal village of Uculet. Could have come from anywhere, I guess. But not a good sign. Tomorrow morning we reach RS3. Everyone is keeping watch for the Japanese sub.

July 14, 1942: The Captain gave us all strict orders never to repeat what we saw today, and indicated the brass back in Victoria would be conducting extensive interviews when we returned to base. Here's what happened.

Myself, First Mate MacIntyre and Seaman Elliott were summoned to the Captain's quarters for a vague initial briefing — something about radio contact from a radar base being suddenly cut off, and the three of us were supposed to go ashore and reconnoitre the situation, reporting back with hourly radio reports.

With the rising sun we left the *Icarus* in a small skiff and rowed ashore to RS3, a god-forsaken radar installation high on a hill on the deserted coast just north of the fishing town of Uculet.

I knew something was up when we were issued handguns, and with MacIntyre in charge of the crew we set out for the shoreline. The tide was out, it was quite calm, and we rode the waves, beached the skiff easily, and dragged it up to the high water line. At first everything appeared normal until Elliott gave a low cry and pointed south. On a distant sand dune were dozens of silver-grey humps scattered about, looking for all the world like forgotten torpedoes in the early morning mist. MacIntyre lowered his binoculars to say the beach was littered with the corpses of sea lions.

Minutes later we were surprised to see a good-sized rubber dingy tied to a log near the sandy shore. There were no identifying marks on it, but we could see where a series of footprints led up into the trees, and we set out to follow them. We surmised the dingy was used by the radar crew.

We weren't that surprised to find a well-tended trail going up the side of the hill — obviously made by the RS3 personnel — and what might have been a very difficult climb through the pristine rainforest was made easier by big wooden steps and ropes to help us up the steeper bits.

It was apparent the trail had been often used, as the

undergrowth was broken in many places and the odd flat spot was churned with boot prints just beginning to fill with a brackish liquid. The switchback climb was hard and uneventful, except for our final rest period before reaching the top, when Elliott said he thought he saw something glint like aluminum through the fir trees, like looking at the sun through gauze curtains.

We followed his finger up through the tall trees and into the bright blue sky, but could see nothing. Elliott finally disbelieved it himself, and we discounted his vision as the result of the heavy physical exercise. Fifteen minutes later we broke out of the woods and into the broad clearing housing the RS3 operations.

The three buildings were arranged in a slightly semi-circular configuration, with the squat building housing the power generator forward left, the kitchen and barracks to the right, and the big radar screen and bunker to the rear. Elliott ran down a concrete-lined trench to check the generator first, returning almost immediately to say it was still working but the area was deserted.

We moved forward to check the barracks and just before rounding the corner of the power plant my nose picked up the faint dizzy sharpness of ozone. We came around the building and stopped, dead in our tracks. The small oval yard was disfigured almost entirely by a large burned-off doughnut shape, with a small open crater in the middle.

The unscorched areas at the circle's proximity were covered with a fine silver ash and then I noticed a number of whitish mounds fanning through a complete circle around the central crater, which glowed slightly silvery in the morning sun.

The thought came this looked like a giant daisy lying against a matte black background, but instead of flower petals the mounds proved to be the bodies of men. There were eight in all, which was strange because I knew the base was staffed with seven men, and the bodies were arranged on their backs with clock-like precision around the slight central hole, with feet almost touching and arms straight by their sides, their remains facing blankly upward.

Clothing and flesh has succumbed to some intense radiation, but buttons, zippers and armament stood out against the now one-dimensional forms. Elliott burned his fingers trying to pick up what appeared to be a handgun beside one of the bodies, and McIntyre ordered us to leave everything as it was, not to touch anything.

A quick check of the barracks answered no questions. The interior looked like a quick evacuation had taken place, but nothing looked missing. The kitchen was still operational and a big pot of coffee was still warm. We backtracked to the door and when I turned for a last look I noticed our ashy footprints were glowing slightly in the cool darkness of the deserted building.

The only place left to check was the radar complex itself, which stood opposite us. Convection currents were still visible from the centre of the small crater, and it was through this distorted air I realized the radar's rectangular face was not turning through its regular horizontal sweeps, but was pointed straight up into the noonday sky.

We skirted the bodies and approached the radar complex. Elliott and McIntyre announced they were going to split up and search for the station's crew, and I cautiously entered the main control room. It took a moment for my eyes to adjust to the greenish light from the main scope — the equipment looked untouched — and then I noticed the limp body of a technician. He was slumped back in his seat, head dangling back as if he were attempting to see through the concrete ceiling.

The scope in front of him should have been tracking through 180 degrees, but it was stationary and the only blip pulsated dead centre on the screen. I moved around the

Illustration: Paul H. Williams

...the dead man's eyes had a distinctly silvered colouration...

body to check how the controls could have been set to point the radar dish upwards, and from this angle I noticed the dead man's eyes had a distinctly silvered colouration, like a solarized photograph. With each blip on the screen they glowed slightly in response, and before my companions joined me I reached out and shut the poor devil's eyes.

Almost immediately the radar blip pulsated faster, and then moved off quickly to the north. McIntyre had just entered the room and was blinking in the darkness when the wall of electronics seemed to sigh and the screen went blank.

The quiet and darkness were too oppressive for our already taut nerves, and we exited into the sunlight and radioed the *Icarus* we were about to return. We didn't mention what we had found.

The sea lion bodies were attracting a variety of scavengers by the time we hit the beach, and the rubber dingy was where we left it. Once back onboard McIntyre reported our findings to the captain. He wasted no time contacting the proper authorities.

We were told, in no uncertain terms, to keep our mouths shut. No relatives. No friends. No newspapers.

My Uncle Mike's diary contained only two more entries, both recorded within a month of the RS3 episode. The first was on July 27, and was simply a story torn out of the Victoria *Daily Colonist*, reporting the death by drowning of able seaman Frank Elliott, who was fished out of the Esquimalt harbour the day before.

The police passed the incident off as an accident, but Uncle Mike had written, in jerky characters, below the clipping:

"Frank told me two days ago he had been visited by two men, civilians in dark suits, who were asking questions about RS3. He told them to get stuffed or he'd have the service police down their necks. Apparently one got a little lippy but the other calmed him down. Frank said anything they wanted to know could be handled through proper channels, and invited them to bugger off."

The last entry was dated August 12, and reads:

"Received news today the *Icarus* was lost and is presumed sunk with all hands missing after being torpedoed multiple times off the coast of Sooke. McIntyre was on board. I guess I'm the only one left."

RICK MCGRATH is a Canadian writer, editor, designer, and publisher. He began his career as a journalist in 1972 and in 1978 switched to advertising, becoming the Creative Director at a number of Vancouver Agencies and finally the Vice President, Creative Services, for Canada's largest investment dealer.

Rick retired in 2000, continued his rather obsessive interest in the writer JG Ballard, and initiated The Terminal Press in 2013. Since then he has published a meagre total of 22 books.

In 2023 he co-edited, with Maxim Jakubowski, a JG Ballard homage collection of short stories, titled *Reports From The Deep End*, for Titan Books in the UK. He also runs the popular website jgballard.ca and has contributed many articles to the now-defunct ballardian.com.

He currently lives north of Vancouver, British Columbia, in a rainforest beside the Salish Sea. This is his first (and only) collection of short stories.

ALSO BY THE TERMINAL PRESS:

The J.G. Ballard Book 2013
Deep Ends: The J.G. Ballard Anthology 2014
Deep Ends: The J.G. Ballard Anthology 2015
Deep Ends: The J.G. Ballard Anthology 2016
Deep Ends: A Ballardian Anthology 2018
Deep Ends: A Ballardian Anthology 2019
Deep Ends: A Ballardian Anthology 2020
Deep Ends: A Ballardian Anthology 2021
Deep Ends: A Ballardian Anthology 2022
Deep Ends: A Ballardian Anthology 2023

Mike Bonsall - Ballardian Diversions

Dominika Oramus - Grave New World: The Decline of the West
in the Fiction of JG Ballard

Lawrence Russell - Radio Brazil
Lawrence Russell - Outlaw Academic
Lawrence Russell - Temple of the Two Moons

Paul A. Green - Terminal Transmissions

Maxim Jakubowski - Cruising The Coast Of Nostalgia

Don McKay - Gambari

Paul H. Williams - Ocular Distrubances

Rick McGrath - Straight Man: Rock Star Interviews, Reviews & Photos
from the 1970s Underground Press
Rick McGrath - The Disenchanted Forest
Rick McGrath (editor) - Unauthorised Departures